WHY DO YOU DANCE WHEN YOU WALK?

Abdourahman A. Waberi

Translated by David and Nicole Ball

Abuja - London

This edition first published in 2022 by Cassava Republic Press
Abuja – London

© 2019 by Editions Jean-Claude Lattès

Copyright © Abdourahman A. Waberi 2022

English translation copyright © David and Nicole Ball 2022

All rights reserved. No part of this book may be reproduced, stored in a retrieval system, or transported in any form or by any means (electronic, mechanical, photocopying, recording or otherwise), without the prior written permission of the publisher of this book.

The moral right of Abdourahman A. Waberi to be identified as the Author of this work has been asserted by him in accordance with the Copyright, Designs and Patents Act 1988. This is a work of fiction. Names, characters, businesses, places and incidents are either the product of the author's imagination or are used fictitiously. Any resemblance to actual persons, living or dead, events or locales is entirely coincidental.

A CIP catalogue record for this book is available from the National Library of Nigeria and the British Library.

ISBN: 978-1-913175-32-0
eISBN: 978-1-913175-33-7

Cover design: Jamie Keenan
Book design: Deepak Sharma (Prepress Plus)

Printed and bound in Great Britain by Clays
Distributed in Nigeria by Yellow Danfo
Worldwide distribution by Ingram Publisher Services International

INSTITUT FRANÇAIS This book has benefited from the support of the French Institute's Publication Support Programme.

Stay up to date with the latest books, special offers and exclusive content with our monthly newsletter.

Sign up on our website:
www.cassavarepublic.biz

Twitter/Tiktok: @cassavarepublic
Instagram: @cassavarepublicpress
Facebook: facebook.com/CassavaRepublic
Hashtag: #WhyDoYouDanceWhenYouWalk #ReadCassava

*To my mother Safia, my grandmother Jim'aa,
my aunt Gayibo and my father Awaleh.*

'What is most personal is most general.'

Carl Rogers

This book has been selected to receive financial assistance from English PEN's 'PEN Translates' programme, supported by Arts Council England. English PEN exists to promote literature and our understanding of it, to uphold writers' freedoms around the world, to campaign against the persecution and imprisonment of writers for stating their views, and to promote the friendly co-operation of writers and the free exchange of ideas. www.englishpen.org

It all came back to me.

I am that child, swimming between the past and the present. All I have to do is close my eyes and it all comes back to me. I remember the smell of the wet earth after the first rain and the dust dancing in the rays of light. I remember the first time I got sick. I must have been six at the time. Fever lashed out at me for a whole week. Heat, sweat and shivers. Shivers, sweat and heat. My first torments date from that period.

The small hours of a morning, in Djibouti, at the beginning of the seventies. My memory always takes me back to that starting point. Today, my memories are less foggy, as I was able to make strenuous efforts to go back in time and put some order into the jumble of my childhood.

Day and night, from the tip of my toes to the tip of my hair, fever attacked me. One day it would make me throw up. The next day I was delirious. I misunderstood the words and the care my parents were giving me. I misjudged what they were doing. Blame it on pain and my tender age. Fever played with my body the way the little girls in the neighbourhood played with their only rag doll.

For six whole days and nights, I shook. I poured out all the water in my body, stretched out on my mat during the day, and then on my little mattress set directly on the floor in the evening. My temperature rose at nightfall. I cried even louder. I called Mama to the rescue. I was impatient, boiling with rage. I hated it when she left me all alone. Under the veranda, my eyes staring at the aluminium roof. I would cry to the point of exhaustion. Finally Mama would come. But I no longer found the slightest comfort in the arms of my mother, Zahra. She didn't know what to do with me. Do something, quick!

demanded the little voice that took hold of her during those moments of panic.

Then what? Then she would entrust the little bag of bones and pains I was to whomever would appear before her.

Who? Who?

Quick, quick, implored the little voice.

So she threw me like a vulgar package into my grandmother's arms,

or into the arms of my paternal aunt Dayibo who was my mother's age.

or into the lap of a passing maid.

Then into the lap of another woman,

an aunt,

a relative,

or a maid,

or even a neighbour, or some matron who had come to say hello to Grandma.

I was passed like this from arm to arm,

from breast to breast.

But I kept on crying,

from pain,

from anger

out of habit, too.

Dawn would arrive, most often without my knowing it. I would be dropping from exhaustion. I'd sleep a little, sniffling and thrashing about in my sleep. I woke up when the first rays of the sun heated up the aluminium roof. Shivering, I would scream with pain and rage. And wake everybody up.

My mother would jump out of bed and blow her nose at length. Maybe she didn't want me to catch her crying but I could see the flash of panic in her eyes that I had already surprised onto her face.

Outside, the city was already full of life. I could hear the children of Château-d'Eau, my neighbourhood, leaving for school. They sounded joyful, noisy, naughty. Whereas me, I was lying on my mattress. Feverish. I would start sobbing again.

I was waving my fleshless arms around, in vain. Mama was sniffling silently, a flash of panic in her eyes again. She found a way out by throwing me into the arms of the first woman who happened to come by.

Grandma's arms,
or my paternal aunt's arms,
or the neighbour's arms.
Then to another one,
then another.
And the circus would begin all over again.
The little sniffle, the panic, for the flash of an instant.
And I would be passed from arm to arm,
like a bundle of sticks.
Why did Mama hate me so much?

I never dared ask myself that question. Only later did it crawl into my thoughts.

It would lodge in my heart. And hollow out a black hole in it.

Every morning, Mama entrusted me to my grandma. I nicknamed her Cochise when I was a teenager, in homage to the famous Indian chief.

So, Grandma.

She was the supreme chief of the family. She ruled with an iron hand, like an Apache warrior over his scattered troops. Nearly blind as she was, Grandma Cochise stood straight and still behind a veil invisible to others. She was a tall, robust woman with delicate features, but shrunken by age. She could hear, taste and smell better than anyone. Her forehead was devastated by wrinkles, her face more creased than the skin of a chameleon. As soon as she heard my thin voice, she would furrow her brow. She had a keen nose like a sheep dog's and sniffed me out before recognizing me. All she had to do then was stretch out her arms and grab me by the skin of my neck like a cat with her kitten. She would effortlessly pull me back onto her lap. And there was only one thing I could do: settle myself against her and calm down. I had to stay put, without moving, without shedding a single tear. But it was impossible. I was born with moist red eyes. I would quickly break down. And the sanction would fall, implacably, upon my shoulders.

Every sniffle was followed by a dark, threatening look. Every tear by a reprimand. Then strokes of the cane on my skull, my collarbone, my elbows, my toes. She could make me howl in pain with one sharp blow. I would sob and sob until I smothered. The days went by, back then, and they all seemed the same. I would hold my breath. I'd launch out my mind like a lasso and finally collapse from sheer exhaustion in the middle of the morning, asleep at last. Grandma's eyes would settle on the rare passers-by whose steps she had perceived well before they reached us. These men and women never failed to greet the matron, who would nod her head after each greeting.

The passerby: 'How's the little boy doing?'

Her: 'Allah the Most Merciful is watching over him, we have no complaints today.'

The passerby: 'And what about your old bones?'

Her: 'If they creak, it's because they're alive.'

The passerby: 'By all the angels in Heaven, you'll sure bury us all, won't you?'

Her: 'I'm counting on it.'

The bowl of millet I hadn't touched would still lie around for a bit. Fifteen minutes later it made a small neighbourhood boy or girl happy. Grandma, solicited by this one or that one, wasn't scolding me for once. It must have been close to ten when the bustle of the neighbourhood went up a notch. Mama was returning from the market. She'd take a stool, drag it over to the old lady to give her news of a convalescent relative, deliver a message from the local imam, or complain about the rising price of meat. Grandma would listen. Nothing seemed to faze her.

I didn't get so much as a glance from my mother. Huddled at the feet of Grandma Cochise, I was shaking with fever. I resented this mother who kept her distance from my little, stunted body on the mat. I tried to calm down to prove that Grandma was right, and to upset Mama more. I'd watch the people idling in the street from a unique vantage point. I had an unobstructed view of a remarkable landscape: the hardened toenails of my grandmother.

I was 45 when you came into my life, Béa. A child of desire, you took your own sweet time before you arrived on earth with fanfare.

I never had a little cuddly animal made of straw or cardboard when I was a child. I was not a healthy, strong, well-nourished baby like you. I was skinny and sickly. To stop my crying, there was often only one solution, which my mother had discovered totally by chance. Great scientific discoveries like aspirin or pasteurization are the daughters of chance, God knows why. One evening, when she was sick of hearing me moaning, my mother plunged me into a white basin filled with cold water, in the shade of the veranda. Today, I replay this scene in my mind with some emotion. I can feel my body shivering again as I tell it to you. Tears are not very far away.

Before I landed in the basin, my throat was so tight I felt like I was suffocating. The scene always ended the same way: I would shiver with cold as the freezing water softened my skin. If my mother was reduced to this radical solution, it's because she had used up every possible ruse and still couldn't manage to calm down the frightful cry-baby that I was. At night, before setting me down on my little mat, she'd tell me all kinds of stories. Tales about obedient children, others about docile animals or affectionate plants. The stories came one after the other. While the whole city was sound asleep, we were the only two people stirring.

At your birth, Béa, a detail caught my eye: you had big ears, a little like Barack Obama. Your little face was hidden under your long eyelashes. You kicked around a lot. Trembling, I examined your limbs. You were a healthy baby, thank God.

Churned by pain, still in a daze, your mother finally emerged from her foggy state to ask me what the baby's sex was.

And I, proud as a peacock, announced, 'It's a girl!'
And you cried out for the second time.
It had become a habit of yours.
You would yell at the drop of a hat.

You insisted that your mother and I obey you hand and foot. As an explosive mixture, you sure are the all-category champion. To the Swiss-Milanese-Sicilian blood of your mother, you must add my African blood—not lazy at all, for my ancestors were nomads and to this day, they keep beating everyone at running.

At four, you were a smiling little girl, curious and full of energy. You would still shout at the drop of a hat. Margherita watched over you with tender eyes and her expansive, Mediterranean love. With her, you can easily go from laughter to tears, from shouts to songs. You and your mom, you sure make a fine pair! A permanent circus, the two of you together. I try to temper your mother's impulses and your energy to find a happy medium, calm and smooth like the flow of a Batavian river. I almost never succeed. In those instances, all I can do is sulk. I sulk, but then two voices gang up to pull me out of that state.

When I wasn't out of town for work or abroad, I was the one who had the privilege of taking you to school. And I was the one to bring you back from school at the end of the afternoon. I loved our time together, just you and me walking for 15 minutes to school and back. From the very start of the morning, you asked so many questions. You, little devil of a girl, you seemed to forget that I'm slow. Especially in the morning. I need time before I can rise to your level of conversation. You were four years old and liked to chatter. The noise of the city didn't disturb our tête-à-tête. We were alone in the world. I had eyes only for you, Béa. Ears only for our conversation. A conversation you would liven up with songs and laughter, according to your personal weather.

'Papa, is '*médecine*' a lady doctor?'

'Hmmm...'

'My friend Letitia says that's what it is, for real...'

We'd cross this little part of the 10th Arrondissement, and three streets further on, we'd reach the 9th. Almost every day, we met the same passers-by in a hurry, the same Chinese shopkeepers washing down the doorstep of their bar-tabac, the same little kids in strollers and the same teenage girls on scooters. Anything could become instantly magical to your eyes. The slightest thing captured your attention as soon as you were out of bed. You'd first wave cheerfully and then shout 'Hi, soldiers!' to the four men in battle dress on duty, machineguns in their hands, plodding heavily up and down the street leading to the neighbourhood synagogue. The soldiers would return your greetings, and by then we could feel impatience growing behind our backs. Some pedestrians frowned and others got annoyed because we were strolling along our bit of sidewalk instead of walking at their frenzied pace. Why walk faster when we had our entire life ahead of us? Glued to their cell phones, these people would push and shove everybody on the street as they did in the corridors of the Metro. Nonchalant and chatty on some mornings, we were strangely silent on others. Those moments of complicity were the most special moments of the day.

One morning, on the way to school, you asked me a question and you put the maximum attention and affection in the tone of your voice. I did not anticipate its object, but I knew that question must have a lot of importance for you. And no doubt, for me as well.

You took your time, keeping a long, suspenseful silence. I could feel a little wind of impatience inside me trying to slip out. I tried to look natural. No word was allowed to come out of my mouth as long as you kept quiet. We were very near your school. A crosswalk, then a bike pickup station, and then all we had to do was to cross, walk along the street and enter the building through its bright blue door. Once inside, parents were often surprised by the modest size of the paved schoolyard, but also by the whiteness of the walls, which gave the building an elegant look.

I was beginning to drift from impatience toward the shores of worry. After the silence, you smiled at me as if to put an end to my rising anxiety. Suddenly, you blurted out:

'Papa, why do you dance when you walk?'

'Umm...'

I was not feigning surprise. You tried again.
'Yes, you do.'
I didn't have the strength to protest.
'You dance like this when you walk, see?'
And you showed me what you meant, ostentatiously swaying in front of me. I tried to put some order into my thoughts. I was touched, I had a moist veil before my eyes. And the distinct impression that the walls of Paris were sending your words back into my ears. I felt a touch of cruelty in your words, Béa. The ancient nomads in my genealogical tree say that truth comes out of the mouths of children and there is gratitude in the eyes of the cow who has just given birth to a calf. That old adage, which I used to find foolish, never seemed so true as it did that morning. You, my little girl, you were sending me back the truth with a dose of affection tinged with gentle firmness.

Your words kept whirling around in my head.
I could no longer shy away from them.
On the last stretch on the way to your school, I nodded at a parent. You tugged at the sleeve of my jacket to signal you had recognized the parent who was in a hurry. My brain had just spun around and returned to your question. And I wondered why I've been dancing all these years when there was only one thing to do.

One thing,
just one.
Walk,
walk straight,
like everyone else.
When I was about to open the door of the school, you must have sensed the turmoil inside of me because you started talking again, but in a lighter tone.

'Papa, you know how to ride a scooter?'
'Maybe... I never tried.'
'Papa, you know how to ride a bike? Like Mom!'
'...'
'*I* know how to ride a bike. But I never saw *you* on a bike.'

The old photo yellowed with age was Margherita's idea. She wanted me to introduce you to my parents and grandparents. It was a nice present for your fifth birthday. And you played along. You went through the different characters one by one. I was not surprised when you said: 'Papa, did you see? Your Mom is really short.' Was that your first comment? Nothing else to point out as you stared at the old picture. *D'accordo*, as your fanciful mother would say, I must admit you're not wrong about my mother's height. When I was small, I had a problem with it. For years, I told myself I could have been tall and strong like a Viking... if only my mother had not been closer to a Pigmy than a Viking. Every evening, I would hop up and down for ten minutes before going to bed because Kassim, a tall oaf of nine on rue Paul-Fort, told me trees use this technique to befriend the skies. My jumping around like a jack rabbit had no result. As I grew up, I was obliged to swallow this humiliation along with many others. You'll see, Béa, you'll swallow some too, one day or another. That photo was only a first step. You wanted to know your ancestors, you were right. You nagged me day and night so I would talk about my parents.

I'm going to tell you about the land of my childhood. And you'll get all the stories that marked my childhood years. I will tell you about my old parents. I will tell you about my past and I will answer your question. I'll tell you about the shifting desert around Djibouti, my native city. I'll tell you about the Red Sea. I'll tell about my neighbourhood and its little houses with corrugated aluminium roofs. You may find it poor and dirty and maybe you won't dare admit it to me. The last time I went there, it really was very dirty. There weren't as many of those damned pieces of plastic littering the alleys of my youth.

Who did you recognize right away in the picture? Zahra, my mother and your grandmother. I know you saw her first in a photo. Then you met her in the flesh at my younger brother's Ossobleh's place, your uncle in Bordeaux whom you adore. How old were you at the time? Two and a half? Was her mouth partially toothless then? That woman was my one and only goad for a long time, can you imagine? The centre of my attention. My love, and my terror, too.

Suddenly, you grabbed the picture out of my hands and brought it up close to your chubby face. And then, close to your eyes, as if you wanted to magnify every line and every grain of my parents' skin. I think I saw a tear on your cheek. You were stroking my father's face with your finger. Papa Beanpole, as I used to call him when I was a child, was standing up, tall and straight as an arrow. Dignified and handsome. About thirty years old. A thin moustache, typical at the time. He was wearing well-pressed khaki pants and a long-sleeved shirt. The absence of colour flattened the checkered motif of his buttoned-up shirt and emphasized the two folds of his pants, which went down to his shining black shoes, lit up by a few whitish spots. He held his head straight; his features looked relaxed and his eyes were staring at the camera. He had probably obeyed the local photographer, who was used to printing the great and small joys of everyday life on film. You noticed that he wasn't really smiling. How could I explain that selfies and social networks didn't exist in your grandfather's time and people were as solemn as a child at his first communion before the bent-down photographer. If your grandfather ever had the wild idea of making faces in the photographer's studio, he would have been dismissed on the spot and advised to go horse around at a rival photographer's place. No bare chests, no bikini, no sandals. In hot countries, people dress from head to toe. Only Westerners strip naked as soon as they feel the slightest ray of sun warming up their skin.

Papa worked a lot.

Far from our house.

Far from the native quarters of the city.

He sold trinkets to the French and to the rare foreign tourists. His little shop, cluttered with statuettes, Moroccan carpets, baskets and other wickerwork items, was located in Quartier 1, at the edge of the real administrative and business city. The upper, white city. At that time, there was a big hospital in that part of Djibouti with all the essential services, including a morgue. Whites, Arabs, and Blacks like us walked alongside each other in the street shoulder to shoulder. At the head of all those people was a White called the High Commissioner. He wore a white uniform and a white kepi decorated with a little blue and red ribbon so that everyone understood he was the big chief. Not only the chief of the Whites, but also of the Arabs, and the Blacks like our family. I understood all that years later, when I passed through the gate of the Collège de Boulaos, the Middle School.

Late at night, Papa would return from work. Hardly had he crossed the doorstep when Grandma Cochise would jump up and pronounce his first name, stretching it out like a rubber band.

Aaaammmmiiiinnnneeee!

As if she were suddenly releasing all the words she had saved up during the day. It was her personal way of telling us she was now reassured and would soon go to bed. Like an Apache chief, she was sounding the horn that meant the end of all activity.

Grandma was more than a little proud of her son Amine, even if she tried to hide that feeling, but that was out of her control—a control otherwise so effective. At that time, I didn't know Grandma could feel admiration for anyone except the bearded Prophet and the old totems of our ancestors.

Late at night, I too was on the lookout for Papa's arrival. I waited for him like the messiah. A familiar, motorized messiah.

At last, I would hear him arrive,

like in a dream.

Papa Beanpole was no longer far away.

My father's arrival was signalled by a series of noises, each more distinct than the last. For miles around, in the cool of the night, we could hear his moped spluttering. Then came the squeal of the brakes, filling my heart with joy, little whiner though I was. And then, his steps would resound in the courtyard. The noises in the bathroom reached me very clearly. The sucking sound of the plastic pipe connected to the faucet. The water flowing by fits and starts into the basin and going tock-tock-tock. So Papa was taking his shower after a long day and evening of work.

My father's presence had a calming effect on everyone. Once she had cried out his name, Grandma would fall back into her usual state of stupor. My mother would be busy in the corner that served as a kitchen and smelled of gasoline. She'd come out with a dish of beans and tomatoes, or chickpea soup bathing in clarified butter. It was close to ten when Mama delicately set the plate of beans and the baguette in front of the stool on which my father sat after his shower. In my memory, I can see him uncomfortably seated on his stool, which would have been more suitable for a teenager. In my memory, I can see Papa Amine again cutting the baguette in half, holding one end of it in one of his hands and slipping the other end under his stool, his legs spread wide apart, his knees grazing his cheeks, while his back stayed very straight.

You've already understood, Béa, that my father was tall and thin. He used to say he was almost as tall as General de Gaulle and my mother was shorter than the general's wife, whom the French affectionately called Aunt Yvonne. Papa would add that he knew a lot of people who felt a boundless affection for

Madame de Gaulle, in our country, too. He would teach you, if you had been lucky enough to bounce on his thighs, that the Gaullists here at home were as numerous as the big black stones in the Djibouti desert. They sometimes felt more French than the French of France, and yet they had never seen the Eiffel Tower or worn a veteran's uniform. They felt they were the sons and daughters of the TFAI and proudly set themselves apart from the people who, here at home, had the status of temporary residents and came to us from neighbouring countries like Somalia, Ethiopia or Yemen. Legally, those people remained foreigners and the military could expel them from one day to the next. But us, your grandfather would add, we were the real children of the TFAI and we were lucky enough to bequeath our status to our children and to their children.

TFAI—that's the name our country had when I was an infant. *Territoire français des Afars et des Issas.* The French Territory of the Afars and Issas.

You first saw your grandmother Zahra in a photo, then you had the pleasure of meeting my mother, 'short on her paws,' as you say mischievously. You met Amine Beanpole, your departed grandfather, virtually. Were you surprised by his old, spluttering motorbike? And finally, my grandmother, with her look of an Indian great sachem. No picture remains of her, so you'll have to imagine her features. Her aquiline nose can spur you on.

I spoke to you of those three people and slipped in, here and there, a smell, a sensation or a word coming to me from the country of childhood. When I talk with you, I realize that everything is coming back to me in the present, vividly, in a sensual way. Like in a movie where the scenes go by in no particular order. Whether the story of the film begins at the ending or in the middle of an episode, it doesn't alter the quality of my memories. I have clear images imprinted on my brain.

My father's smell, for example,

a mixture of sweat, benzine and cold tobacco.

Not forgetting the sounds of the night.

Or the rustling of the butterflies.

Or the dance of the gecko beneath the pale neon light hanging in the middle of the little courtyard.

Every evening my faithful, reliable gecko would be there, dancing for me, or dancing because that's all it knows how to do.

It was dancing when I was crying, far from my mother's arms.

It is said that every creature holds a secret.

Every secret has its key.

It will appear before your eyes sooner or later.

Once again, I can see my father coming out of the bathroom. A dark, cramped room with a hole in the middle; they call it 'Turkish toilets'—God knows why!

It always went the same way. My father would come out of the bathroom. His steps were lighter, he had taken off his black shoes and put on goatskin sandals, like the ones our nomadic ancestors wore long ago. I could finally hear the sound of his voice. A basso continuo. 12 or 15 minutes earlier, he had announced that he was leaving to 'get wet'; that was his word for 'wash up.' Refreshed and stripped to the waist, he would return in silence.

My heart would be pounding.
I wanted him to lean over me.
To stroke my cheek.
Calm my fears.
Take me in his vigorous arms.
Murmur a few words in my ear.
Confide something to me—a secret, perhaps.
'Come, Papa. Come, Papa!'
'Come quickly, Papa!'

My call had no effect whatsoever. His silence increased my rage tenfold. A few steps more and he'd glance for the last time at his Seiko watch. He would then enter the master bedroom and drop onto his big bed. And soon, he'd be asleep. Snoring. And I would burst into tears.

Mama scolded me. She said I mustn't bother him with my crying, my whims and my sighs. But I didn't listen to anybody. Especially not to her.

The tears flowed by themselves.
My throat knotted up all by itself.
My eyes had been red my whole life.
I had to cry, and that was that!

The last character is right in front of you, Béa. No need for an old sepia photo. We have hundreds of pictures of you and me saved in the memory of the family computer and available in two or three clicks.

I'm going to introduce myself just for form's sake or, let's say, to better inhabit my role as a storyteller. My name is Aden Robleh. But for the children in my neighbourhood, I was Puny or Little Runt. For a long time, these jeers served as my identity card. That past was my prison. From now on, I want to send it back in the distance. Free myself from it. It's because you asked me a question that means a lot to me that the past came back with such freshness. That's why I'm sharing it with you, my sweet Béa. It took a long time before it rose to the surface again. Before it emerged from the mist in the early hours of the morning. Today it's not like that anymore. And I have to thank you for it. I must thank the Lord and Satan, too, as both of them cradled my childhood. Every evening, Grandma Cochise prayed copiously to the former to deliver me from the claws of the latter. 'So much fever... This child is really unlike the others!'

My name is Aden because I was the first child of the Robleh family. The only child for a good long time. For seven whole years, before the arrival of my younger brother Ossobleh, I was the prince of the kingdom but I didn't know it. I was just a ball of pain, of tears and cries. Fears as dense as thickets filled my nights. In the city of my childhood, there was always a lot of sun and dust. I couldn't stand the scratches of the sun, and the dust ravaged my asthmatic lungs.

For a long time, I groaned under insults and jeers. I was incapable of defending myself. I didn't have the strength. All the kids knew that already, or rather, they could tell right away. I kept out of the way. Fearful and shy, I didn't feel whole like the others, who had no problem pushing me around. They must have thought my skeleton was made of plaster. Some of them imagined I carried a secret on my shoulders that was too heavy to bear. The boldest of them asked me senseless questions and I would just sniffle in silence. Back then, I was weak and feverish for no medical reason.

It was in my nature.

I stayed on my guard.

But I was animated by an irresistible force that their childish minds couldn't fathom. I had eyes only for the teacher, I had ears only for her. She was putting me, the little misfit, into orbit.

For a smile from Madame Annick, I would do anything.

Raise my head, run through the covered schoolyard, risk my life.

Face the worst hoods of the Château-d'Eau school, the seismic centre of my quarter. At the time, the word 'quarter' only applied to us, the natives, who lived in the lower city, the African city crowded with most of the 250,000 inhabitants of the TFAI.

I'm repeating myself; I know. Madame Annick monopolized all my attention.

Madame Annick was a Frenchwoman.

But get this: a Frenchwoman from France.

A Frenchwoman from France, blonde with eyes the colour of emeralds.

A Frenchwoman from *la belle France*, beautiful France, rich, green and rainy, nothing like our territory of France that was not rich, not green, not rainy, but hot, dry, and rich in black pebbles. We were little Frenchmen who had never seen France. Yes, Béa, I swear, it sounds weird today in the era of mass tourism but that's the way it was before. When you were five, you'd taken the plane twenty-five or thirty times. But in the TFAI, aside from career military and draftees, the natives very rarely took a plane. That's why I thought Madame Annick was so different from us.

And first of all, she lived in a real house, a permanent structure, or maybe in an apartment house on the Plateau du Héron in the most modern part of the city. The higher part belonged to the French-from-France, the lower part to the natives.

Madame Annick must have left the Territory the year I turned 12, which coincided with independence, celebrated in June 1977. One day, when I got out of school, I decided to follow Madame Annick. Just to see. For days on end, I prepared various stratagems but I hit a snag. Yet the obstacle was there, right under my eyes, Béa, but for some strange reason, I hadn't thought of it. The teacher was returning home at the wheel of her little car. Nobody around me had a car. My father was the only one in our sector who had a moped but he came back late at night and would be totally against tailing Madame Annick when she left school to return to the upper city through Rue des Issas and Place Arthur-Rimbaud.

Maybe Madame Annick lived on the coast road and if that was the case, she might go around Place Rimbaud by the Boulevard des Salines. From where she lived, on the Plateau du Serpent or the Plateau du Marabout, she could hear the waves breaking on the rocks. If she lived in the Héron, the waves were the same, but they were on the other side of the bay. On the Marabout plateau, still other waves, still similar yet very different. The sector called Quartier Brière-de-L'Isle was where the cream of the French-from-France lived and it had the particularity of including all the barracks of the 5th Overseas Inter-arms regiment based in our country, Djibouti. The only time I set foot there was around 1979 or 1980, when I turned

14. I came back from there dumbfounded. I had no idea that, just a few years earlier, our parents could not walk around that neighbourhood at night unless they worked there as guards, gardeners or cooks, in which case they had a pass duly signed by their employer.

Only Madame Annick counted for me back then.

She had emerald eyes, like the water of a clean pool. Diaphanous eyes like the sky on a clear day.

Sometimes her blonde hair would rise on top of her skull and she'd flatten it with creams and various pomades. She had rebellious tufts of hair, she would sigh in the schoolyard. Unlike us, the natives. No one here in Djibouti had rebellious hair. Not even Askar, the neighbourhood madman. His thick, tangled tresses were covered with filth as if some kids had poured the contents of the Hôtel Ménélik's dumpster on his head and made a point of renewing the operation every day of the week.

Madame Annick often wore a bright blouse and a sand-coloured skirt, held at the waist by a thin, black belt. She had a golden ring and silver bracelets that clinked together as soon as she moved her sun-tanned arms. I admired her strong legs when she walked around the classroom. I couldn't take my eyes off her nicely shaped calves, her white socks and her supple, comfortable sandals. Everything about her was admirably in its place.

Her back arched, her head bent slightly forward, the palms of her hands resting on her desk, that was the position in which Madame Annick started every school day. I'll fast forward the episode of our arrival in the schoolyard. The shoves, the insults and sometimes the spit I'd wipe off discreetly without looking the kid who'd done it in the eye. And then, the principal arrived in the middle of the yard to pull the rope that unleashed a heavy, metallic sound that still resonates in my ears over forty years later. After that, we lined up single file in silence and waited for the teacher to ask us to go into the classroom. Still single file and in the strictest silence. She'd begin the morning by calling the roll. My heart would beat harder and harder as the letters of the alphabet went by.

Now she was reciting the names in L, M, N, O and P. And there I was, in a state of feverish excitement, my body swaying violently forward and back all by itself, like a hamster confined in its cage. I heard the clicking of the briefcases opening in rhythm. The school was a sanctuary. I felt protected by the teacher. I was honoured to be called on by Madame Annick.

'Rabeh!'
'Ragueh!'
The earth stopped rotating.
It was my turn.
'Robleh!'
I couldn't manage to get a word out of my mouth.
Madame Annick would raise her head. Her eyes met mine.
And then, deliverance.
'Aden Robleh!'
'Here, Madame!'
I could breathe again.
My puny little body would finally relax.
The school day couldn't have started better.

I never knew why Johnny had humiliated me in front of everybody on the first day of school. Mama had dressed me in an adorable little boy's outfit. A white shirt with blue sleeves. Khaki shorts. Sandals, and a pair of oxblood-coloured socks. Maybe Johnny didn't like my socks. Or maybe he wanted to pass on the message to all the pupils that this year he would be even more pitiless than all the previous years. But why was I the sacrificial victim? I will never know, Béa.

It was the first day of school. The racket of recess had disrupted my inner compass. The other kids had rushed out of class and were now running all over. They were insulting each other copiously, cursing the mother of this one and the grandmother of another. I kept out of it. Nobody had come to play with me and that was perfectly fine. The teachers were chatting in the meeting room. Madame Annick had gone off to say hello to the principal and her colleagues in her office, where you could admire a map of France with every *département* and every territory represented in a different colour. By poring over this map for years, Béa, like you when you examine the old photos of your father's family, I learned strange names that had a delicate resonance to the ears of the second grader that I was: Alsace, Auvergne, Charente-Maritime. Guadeloupe. Réunion...not forgetting our dear TFAI. In short, on this first day of school, the discussion in the meeting room was dragging on a little longer than usual because the adults had vacation memories or pedagogical instructions to share. So recess stretched on. I was impatiently waiting for the bell to sound. But nothing was forthcoming.

The urge to run across the schoolyard suddenly crossed my mind. That way, I would take the time to admire the fruits of the jujube tree that had fallen and no one had thought to pick up, no doubt because they were all dry and inedible. But then, seeing the mob camped in the middle of the yard, I gave up on my bold plan. The bell still was not ringing. Mustering all my courage, I began to run toward the jujube tree. Between the leafy green tree and the covered part of the yard from where I had dashed was the fountain, just behind the classroom of the fifth graders, the oldest kids in the school, the responsibility of Monsieur Émile Trampon, who also served as principal. Suddenly, Johnny surged out from behind the third-grade classroom and came running toward me. My heart was beating so hard I could feel it drumming in my ribcage.

What was going to happen to me? You're wondering too, Béa. Did he just want to quench his thirst, like me? Did that good-for-nothing have another idea at the back of his mind?

I was right next to the fountain. So was Johnny. I had the time to feel his breath on the nape of my neck, to see his slightly asymmetrical eyes and his murderous smile. Now he was in my back. He had taken his time to go around me. *He's letting me through*, I thought. All I had to do was lean over the faucet and drink the water collected in the palm of my right hand. And then it was my head that hit the faucet. Blood was flowing freely, mixing into the water. Adults came running. Someone picked me up. I was crying my eyes out. My eyebrow was cut open, my right cheek and my nose were scraped, my knee was bleeding a lot. I was writhing from the pain. From distress, too. It wasn't the shock that was bothering me but the violence of the fall I took when he tripped me. And above all, the spectacle of my humiliation on the very first day of school.

That fall would follow me for years. Johnny, my tormentor, was proud of himself. Having reaffirmed his role as a leg-breaker, he had no more worries about keeping his crown. As for me, I was to remain wimpish and docile. On the watch all year long, I would jump every time I heard the sound of his voice and then his throaty laugh. I did all I could to avoid his squinty, shifty looks. You can get punched so quickly! And tripped, too.

They called him Johnny and I never learned his real name. An older neighbour must have found that nickname in a comic strip collected from a trash can. Unless his tough, manly old man meant to pay tribute to some ferocious dog guarding the villa of a superior officer or to Johnny Hallyday, the rock 'n' roll French star venerated by all the draftees and officers of the TFAI. Johnny's father didn't squint like his son, but something wasn't quite right with him either. He was followed by a pack of hangers-on all day long. At night, the gang of merry noisemakers would roar out its concert, demanding the share of bushmeat Johnny's father owed them. He had kept that habit from his past, when he was a member of the famous military corps, the GNA (three easy letters to remember). As children, we knew nothing of that *Groupement Nomade Autochtone*, composed exclusively of natives, and its exploits to counter the raids of our enemies and keep our borders inviolate and inviolable.

Tall, fat and strong, the father spent his time combing his slicked-down hair, which he kept long, like the effeminate, waddling Arabs. He worked in a barbershop frequented by French soldiers from the mother country or its overseas territories and *départements* to learn parachute jumping in the desert or swimming in the turquoise sea in the midst of the bull sharks. They call that toughening exercises and it would seem the Lord or Satan was intent on making our little country the best terrain for this type of exercise. That's why the Gaullists and superior officers (they're often the same) love to trek around the mountains of Goda and Mabla, on the hills of Arta or in the crater of Goubet, which goes down deep into the bowels of the earth.

In the schoolyard, Johnny acted like a drill sergeant. He barked at the guys in his troop who followed him everywhere. As soon as they had gone through the gates of the school, their movements became coordinated and they spoke in one voice. Johnny would give an order and his underlings hastened to execute it. The first one to carry out the task was noisily congratulated by the ogre who held him up as an example. And if, the next day, he failed, the poor wretch would return to anonymity. Which was considered a horrible punishment.

My celebration of the first day of school was ruined. I deserved a better fate, but Johnny had decided otherwise: he gave me the role of a victim just good enough to make fun of. Or worse still, to shove or hit.

When I got home, Mama asked me how my first day had gone. Great! I lied. On the way back, I had succeeded in enumerating the number of days I would have to spend at school, while quickening my pace and watching my back for fear of coming across the squint of Wicked Johnny again.

After a weary sigh, Mama examined my face with an inquisitive eye. She had sensed that something wasn't right but she wasn't absolutely sure. I did nothing to help her. Persisting in my lie, I began to whistle a little tune of my own invention. Without realizing it, I was imitating the grownups who put on an air of importance as they go through the alleys of our Château-d'Eau neighbourhood at night. I smiled at Mama. For once. To fool her. To keep my pain inside too. My pain is a desert island, I thought, deep inside myself. It cannot be shared.

To this day, I can't explain why I persisted in lying to Mama. Johnny made me suffer unjustly and her words would have mended my heart. But for that, I needed to confide my pain to her first.

Mama's fear was not unfounded. My knee really had been badly scraped. It had bled abundantly and I had trouble bending it. I went hopping around all day. The nurse who had taken care of me gave Mama precise instructions: disinfect the wound with alcohol and mercurochrome, apply an ointment, and change the dressing twice a day. Moreover, she had to make me drink abundantly to avoid getting dehydrated and make me eat correctly. Check to see if my immunization record was up to date. Mama agreed without taking her eyes off my wound. Suddenly, fear took hold of her. She knew, of course, that I had a fragile constitution and had never been vaccinated. The faucet of the fountain was made of grey metal. Bronze or iron. Or an alloy of other metals. The risk of tetanus could not be ruled out.

Mama ran to the clinic and came galloping back. But not empty-handed. I suddenly felt the bite of alcohol on my open wound. With a shaky hand, Mama cleaned out the pus and spread tincture of iodine on my knee; it was supposed to drive off the bacteria and their morbid miasmas. All she had to do now was to wrap the dressing around my little knee. After that, she began massaging my calf and shinbone. It lasted a long time. I could feel her fingers trembling. I knew at this moment that Mama was afraid of death. Old feelings were assailing her. In her distant family, she'd had paralytic relatives, blind people and still others who dragged around stumps eaten away by leprosy. I was then her only child. Fragile and sickly, to boot. She was protecting me in her own frightened and disorganized way. My infected wound could have infiltrated my body without her knowledge. She had no way of knowing. She felt guilty. Guilty to her fingertips. Guilty to the bone.

In our neighbourhood, death had a familiar face.

It struck hard.
It struck often and indiscriminately.
One day that fate would descend on an infant.
Another day an old man would give up the ghost.
Families hit by drought would drag themselves to our city with their guts on fire.
With their mouths open and a cloud of flies over their faces.
They relieved themselves wherever they could.
The city was surrounded by a putrid, animal odour.
The health authorities and even the military feared an outbreak of cholera.
Was it too late already?
From contamination to contamination, the epidemic was finally reaching the capital. Dysentery and cholera hit the Territoire in cycles and the nomads whose flocks had died from the drought in the sub-region retreated to the villages and hamlets of the TFAI. Scared stiff, the French-from-France kept away. They peed in their pants or in their military boots. The High Commissioner of the Republic asked Paris for help. But no miracle in sight. New families poured in from the bush in waves. Weakened by illnesses, the adults were dragging behind their rickety children, followed by swarms of flies. The two or three clinics of the capital could not deal with such a scourge. The families from the bush didn't have the strength to return and were struck down in a week. People said their corpses were kept for a time in the morgue and then covered with acid powder before they were dumped into a mass grave if no one showed up to claim them.
Mama lived in fear of meeting death. Her worst nightmare: seeing me carried away by the Grim Reaper. She'd get up in the middle of the night to inspect my jaws. Were they flexible or contracted? Was my torso rigid? Stomach pains? Was my throat sore? My glands swollen? My limbs inert? Neck stuck, yes or no? Did I pee often and abundantly? Was I sleeping enough? Now, how come I wasn't crying as much as I used to? Where did my fever go? And what about my asthma? Was I

coughing a lot? If so, during the day or at night? Wet or dry, the cough? Any bloating, flatulence? Was I getting weak-kneed?

That's how she was, my mother. Fearful, superstitious. She never stopped imagining the worst. As soon as a morbid thought trotted through her mind, she'd stride off to the chief of the family, who had the reputation of having the science of darkness at her fingertips. And Grandma Cochise would scold her, reminding her that only the Lord or Satan had the last word and she shouldn't worry herself sick over a cold or a little stomach ache. Once she was reassured, Mama would retreat into funereal silence, from which she would only emerge at the triumphal arrival of a new thought, disturbing for her but a mystery for the rest of the family. At the time, I was unaware of this whole side of Mama's personality, as my main terror was more concrete. It resided in my school. It was lodged in the classroom next to mine. It lighted a cigarette with a heavy, metallic Zippo in the schoolyard to taunt the adults. It would draw on the cigarette, cough, draw on the cigarette and cough again. Its face did not wear a pirate mask but a squint that was just as terrifying. My terror had an exotic male name. You guessed it, Béa. Its name was Johnny.

Madame Annick had an advantage over everybody else I knew. She could read and write French. As I told you, Béa, Madame Annick was a Frenchwoman from France. Not only did she know how to read and write but she knew that language very well, well enough to come all the way to us, to our country, and transform the great-grandsons of nomadic shepherds like me into little boys who knew how to read, write and count. They had to enter the modern world and succeed better than their parents. The French Republic had given her this sacred mission. All the little children, blond or black, must be educated to get a good position in life afterwards. *Liberté, égalité, fraternité* for all. Even for dogs. In reality, things were not so simple. Our parents had been overlooked by Madame Annick's former colleagues. The ones who came from the mother country to educate them when Papa and Mama still had a chance of learning to read, write and count in French.

I'm not ashamed to say that my father couldn't read or write French.

Mama couldn't read or write French.

Grandma Cochise couldn't read or write French.

My aunt, all my cousins, boys and girls, my uncles, my grandparents and even the neighbours—all those folks couldn't read or write French.

Only Madame Annick could teach me how to read and write French.

Askar the Madman could read and write French but Askar was a strange character. First of all, he was dirty as a pig, Madame Annick would have said. He talked to himself and ate the food he picked out of garbage cans. You could recognize him from a distance. From a great distance. All you needed was your nose. Askar gave off a smell of cow dung and nomad poop mixed together. I didn't know one single person who could stay near Askar for more than two seconds. When Askar slowly walked toward the gate of our school, everybody ran away. Johnny and his gang of slobs would insult him and bombard him with stones. Askar didn't even notice what they were up to. He kept moving slowly forward, like a ship coming back to port. He dragged along his elephantine legs, his ragged clothes and his enormous bundles.

People said Askar had been an important man. He could speak and write French. He had worked in an air-conditioned office for years. He had a whole bunch of people under his orders, some of them French-from-France. Every office day, he'd put on a fine white shirt, buttoned all the way up, a pair of black pants and black, well-polished shoes. He left his house in his car. Yes, I did say house, Béa, because he lived in a real house, not like us in the outer quarters. Once he entered his office, a secretary would greet him with a phony smile and a steaming cup of coffee. Askar then sharpened his pencils before getting to work. He always kept two well-sharpened pencils in his shirt pocket.

Ah, I forgot to tell you, Béa: before leaving the house, Askar would kiss his wife. At the time, there were different opinions about how to describe this sort of kiss. Half of TFAI claimed that the only senior civil servant to have risen from our native ranks kissed his wife on the mouth. The other half retorted that all he did was graze the cheek of his European wife and Askar had neither forgotten nor rejected our nomadic roots. Both parties, however, agreed that he stroked the heads of his twin girls named Olivia and Viola for some time. Then, before getting into his car, also white except for its black roof—he started up the engine and took the time to let it heat up. After that, he honked his horn to say goodbye to his nice family who, from the marble steps in front of their house, wished him an excellent day.

In our neighbourhood, the days were all alike. Nobody wished me an excellent day or a good nap. Nobody celebrated birthdays and the date of birth on my birth certificate gave me no right to anything at all. I celebrated my birthday for the first time in France, when I turned 22. I see you look surprised, dear girl, but that's how things were in the kingdom of my childhood. I can understand you: we never missed a single one of your birthdays, from the first to the seventh.

Things were different in my neighbourhood. Mind you, I'm not complaining. There was nothing unusual about my situation. No gifts, no cake. Even the notion of a birthday, with its rituals, songs and festivities, would have seemed useless to us. Silly, too. Relations with parents were distant. Respectful, but distant. Each group knew its place. Us—the neighbourhood kids—were all in the same boat. Many of us spent our time running through the alleys like thirsty goats or shrieking like little baboons. Like dazed owls, we saw our parents again in the evening when the sun had gone to bed behind the mountain of Ambouli. At that time, the gate of the school had long been closed and Madame Annick must have been bathing her children. I had no idea, but I liked to think of her as an attentive, affectionate mother. When night fell in the neighbourhood, the adults would leave their shack to take the air after a scorching hot day. Groups would gather spontaneously between two rows of houses. People came together to listen to the crackling radio.

One evening, the grownups had squabbled a lot after listening to the radio. A young man, skinny as a rail but with well-groomed hair, was telling them excitedly how the Americans had sent a man to the moon.

'It was exactly one year ago!' he vociferated, while watching the reaction of his audience.

A fat bearded man got up in one bound, grabbed the skinny but well-groomed young man and scolded him as if he were a kid in Johnny's insolent gang.

'Young man, you're innocent as the ox and the donkey in our old fables. The Americans are big liars—learn that once and for all!'

'Yes, nothing but big liars,' repeated the other adults, nodding their heads.

The fat bearded man was visibly pleased with his act. His arms made big circles in the air as if he wanted to redraw in the sky the path of the moon, the stars and the sun that had hidden itself behind the big mountain of Ambouli.

'If the Americans were telling the truth, all they had to do was paint a piece of the moon green. That way, we could see it from far away,' an old man said between his clenched teeth.

I did not find the old man's verdict so strange. It also had the advantage of appealing to most of the people. For me, it was the first time I heard the word 'American'. I didn't know if it meant people like the French-from-France or a herd of wild buffaloes. As soon as grownups were squabbling in front of the radio at night, you could be sure that sooner or later they'd say words like 'Americans,' 'nuclear bomb,' 'de Gaulle,' 'Mobutu' or 'Haile Selassie.' I didn't know what they were talking about yet. The clamour of their voices was as heavy as a tropical storm that had picked the wrong season to drench the corrugated aluminium roofs of our neighbourhood. The scent of acacia floated over those makeshift roofs, the smell of ploughed earth rose in the sky, carried along by a sea breeze, and finally, light scents of iodine and algae would tickle our noses.

I was almost as old as you are when Mama left home without warning. I was exactly seven years and six months old. Mama had left. For a destination that was kept secret. Grandma Cochise told me sharply that there was no point asking questions.

'None of your business!'

As usual, her decision was final. Luckily, my aunt had intimated that Mama would be back fairly soon.

'How soon?'

'Two or three days, if all goes well!'

I decided to hang around the house and not stick so much as a toe outside as long as Mama wasn't back. I couldn't just twiddle my thumbs: I had a sort of premonition. Madame Annick's voice and emerald-green eyes didn't monopolise my thoughts as they had the previous semester, inaugurated as it was with the humiliation that horrid Johnny had inflicted on me before everyone. I spent most of my time thinking about death. Learning how to die was a constant preoccupation of mine. A vast subject for reflection. I know it's true for you, too, Béa. You ask me tons of questions about death, disappearance, the world after death. *What happens when you are dead?* you ask. As a matter of fact, I, too, used to wonder where my dead grandparents and their grandparents could have gone. Where were they hidden? Why didn't they visit us anymore? What had the Lord or Satan done, so we didn't hear about them anymore? If they weren't detained somewhere—in a German bunker, perhaps—surely they would have contacted us. They were polite before they died, right? Politeness demanded that you take the time to introduce yourself to your great-grandchildren born, like me, after their departure. I would have been glad to be introduced to them. They would have told me a few secrets about the mystery of their disappearance. Name, profession, details about the illness that had carried them off. For the ones who had died in an accident: day, place and circumstances. In short, how did they all die? And what were their reactions? Did they burst into tears or faced up to the sharpened sabre of the Grim Reaper? Those were the questions that crossed my mind. I know they're going through your mind, too, now, at this particular stage of your existence.

After Mama left, the house was plunged in deep silence. My aunt and I communicated only through occasional sighs. Every time Grandma Cochise had her back turned, one of us would give out an almost inaudible moan. My aunt didn't have the same fears as I did but it was her way of supporting me and in truth, her method was neither better nor worse than any other. At that moment, I really appreciated it. At least one grownup showed me a few signs of attention and affection. Grandma kept her silence and her secrets to herself. And why did Mama leave without a word to me, her only son?

I had no friends and Moussa, my classroom neighbour, wasn't talking to me anymore. I didn't have a girlfriend either, of course. You're going to laugh at me, Béa, but I don't remember talking to a girl once in all my years at the Château-d'Eau school. I was shut tight, like an oyster. Grownups who spoke to me only got a murmur or a gurgling sound in reply. As soon as someone came near me, my throat tightened and my larynx sank to the bottom of my chest. My lips opened and closed but no sound would come out of them. My sullenness, my inaudible voice, my swallowed-up words and my wide-eyed stare didn't fool anyone. I had no gift for conversation. Neither did I feel the need to put everything that was hatching inside my head into words. Some people spit out everything that goes through their minds and will unhesitatingly confide their most intimate secrets with the firstcomer. As for me, I'd rather die than confide anything at all. It was in my nature and I made no particular effort to hold myself to this cardinal rule. People avoided me like the plague. They told nonsensical stories about me that were totally untrue. They said I'd spent the first years of my life in a special hospital for disturbed children, a 'sanatorium.' This word is so complicated to pronounce that the children who are sent there must really be sick in the head. To have a healthy mind and body after a passage in the sanatorium was even more unlikely than transforming cow dung into sweet-smelling flowers.

I was still waiting for my mother to return. My father was coming home later and later. The charm of his spluttering moped was broken. Our neighbours and cousins were growing scarce, as if everybody had spread the word to avoid us. My aunt was getting tired of my bad mood. From afar, they could see my skinny neck and my collarbones moving by themselves. I had learned to sob all alone in my corner without arousing suspicion.

Instinctively, Grandma Cochise knew I was going through a bad period. When I was disappointed or bitter, she guessed it. She admitted later that my upper lip would retract slightly and that's how she could tell people were bitter. They got mad easily and woke up before the others. Worried and fearful, they were always on the alert. They'd jump as soon as a lizard moved its tail on the wall opposite them. I have to confess, Béa, that Grandma had judged correctly once again. I could even say, like the detectives Dupont and Dupond in Tintin comics, that she had hit the bullseye. For an old lady nearly blind, that sure wasn't bad!

Mama came back one afternoon when the sky was smiling. She was not alone. She was transporting something in a small basket protected from the sun by a blanket like those jute cloths used by women from the bush. They came to sell us food that all sons of nomads love: camel's milk, clarified butter, ostrich eggs and strips of dried camel meat with beads of salt on them. The cream of the crop was always diced dromedary humps that looked from afar like ordinary little squares of transparent soap. My father would pick their finest jute cloths to sell to tourists looking for traditional crafts.

In actual fact, Béa, it wasn't exactly a basket but a tiny bassinet, so tiny it seemed to disappear in my mother's arms. The product wrapped up with such precautions was not bush meat or camels' humps to tickle the taste buds of city dwellers nostalgic for the savannah. The ululating cries of the women gave it away: the bassinet did not contain some tasty dish. There was no doubt about it: hardly perceptible sobs were reaching my ears. Mama had cut out for a destination kept secret and now she was back, preceded by signs of attention from all the women in the neighbourhood, who'd come running on some kind of signal that had escaped my vigilance. If we hadn't been in the middle of the afternoon, they could have communicated by means of storm lamps with long wicks, following a sophisticated code too hard for me to decipher. It wasn't because I'd just learned to read, thanks to Madame Annick, that I could easily decode the means of communication used by the women. At any rate, they all participated in that gathering, whether impromptu or planned well in advance. They didn't seem to notice me, so busy were they chanting, inspecting every fold of the skin, every bone and hair of the little creature that my mother, trembling with emotion, was holding in her arms. One matronly woman wiped Zahra's face with a cloth pulled out of her fat chest before wiping her nose, for my mom couldn't possibly let go of the baby for one second, or even give the bassinet to another lady as she usually did with me when I cried so she could blow her nose in peace. Another matronly lady who had just entered the house came over and smacked two big resounding kisses on my mother's tear-streaked cheeks as warm as the sea at Triton beach at the height of the midsummer heat.

.As I watched all these women clustered around the baby newly arrived in our corner of the earth, I understood a little better what we call the maternal instinct that needs no words. Of course, I didn't talk that way then, as you can well guess, Béa, but through intuition I had access to what is at the heart of the relationship between a baby and her mother or father. It seems to me that this type of relationship is completely different from all others we might have known before. Ideal parents expect nothing from their offspring. They're just there for the well-being of their children. For their transformation, their happiness. I must admit it's not the path taken by most of the parents I have known, but this is the path I see myself on, at the side of your mother Margherita, your grandmother Carlotta, your big brothers Yacine and Elmi, and your grandfather Salvatore.

The matronly lady who had come in last was talking with Grandma Cochise, who was redoubling her attentions to my mother. She was scolding her as if she were a little girl and not the wife of her elder son who was also the apple of her eye. My grandmother's name was Nadifa, even if I had never heard anyone call her by her first name. For me, she was Grandma Cochise. She remained Grandma Cochise. For the others, she was the Elder and everyone prayed in silence when they heard her come near. She inspired fear and respect, that's all.

My mother's return attracted a large part of the neighbourhood women. The discussions around her had begun a good hour ago but none of them dared walk away from the bassinet. They stayed there like hens clucking around the mother and her infant while the two old women with emaciated lips conferred with each other on how to penetrate the secrets of life and find the keys of destiny. They were anxious to calm the spirits of the dead before the newborn could utter his first cries inside the house where from now on he would make his poops and his belches and take his first steps. The consultation went on and on, but nobody saw anything to be concerned about it. The hens kept clucking and Mama was sweating like a mozzarella.

By the time the experts in the science of darkness were done conferring, it was almost night. The neighbours left, one after the other, holding a storm lamp at shoulder level. It took me some time to notice that the neighbourhood had been plunged into darkness for over two hours. Had the head mechanic of the EDD, the Djibouti electricity company, forgotten to turn on the general switch? Did the man go sleep off his khat with his head between the thighs of his mistress? Or maybe his assistants didn't have the guts to wake him? Whatever the reason, it was in this slightly magical atmosphere created by the darkness and the hissing of the storm lamps that my little brother uttered his first cry.

I'm usually slow to react, Béa, but I jumped from my seat and flew into the arms of my mother, who kept drying her abundant tears.

I was finally able to check out my new roommate up close.

The skin of his buttocks was supple and wrinkled.

His eyes were close together and his lips were pursed.

He could already moo loud enough to keep my mother under his yoke.

Seeing his legs energetically wriggling about, I could tell my roommate was of a nature different than mine.

He would definitely be as dynamic as I was fragile.

And as vigorous as I was sickly.

The night kept going into overtime; neighbours were taking turns congratulating my father, who had just arrived. For once, I hadn't heard his moped spluttering; my mind must have been elsewhere. The next day, an imam came to bless my roommate.

It was Grandma, of course, who had whispered the baptismal name into the holy man's ear. Aunt Dayibo stayed with the imam all afternoon. After each prayer, she ostentatiously rattled her prayer beads. My mother seemed so frail in her new dress. Papa Beanpole was impeccably dressed in his three-piece suit. And me, my feet were so squeezed inside my shoes that I nearly fainted.

'I am leaving you in very good hands, Ossobleh!'

That's how the imam said goodbye, much to the dismay of my aunt Dayibo, who wiped away a last tear.

'Welcome to the world, Ossobleh!'

That's how, in their turn, the neighbours said goodbye.

'Ossobleh, you will be strong as a rock!'

That's how Grandma ended the ceremony.

I don't remember the rest.

I had gone to bed.

Grandma had forgotten to tell me a story.

Nobody had come to wish me good night.

Ossobleh was bawling in the night.

I was no longer the only son.

My little sister was born just nine months after Ossobleh, my loudmouth younger brother. When she died, I felt even more alone. I was the eldest, but after her death and my mother's period of convalescence, everyone only paid attention to my little brother. And Papa Beanpole, preoccupied with the low returns of his little shop, came home later and later. The house seemed like a hollow shell and the neighbourhood a silent theatre. I was afraid of this silence, as if I had fallen into a dark hole, as if no one had noticed my absence. One evening, as I was rummaging through the trunks piled up in the back of my grandmother's room, I made a surprising discovery. Quite by chance, I fell upon notebooks that had belonged to an old uncle. His name was Aden, too, and I soon learned he had founded a mosque in the backcountry. My parents had given me his name, some nine years earlier, to maintain a kind of connection to this man, much loved in the family, who had died well before I was born. The gossips proclaimed that past the age of 30 I would be squint-eyed, skinny and bald as a billiard ball just like my namesake. I was already skinny, Béa, but not squinty in the least.

Now I could read by myself. I was always on the lookout for some book or magazine to devour. That activity calmed me down greatly. Madame Annick, whom I was delighted to see again, read us long, real stories. The adventures of Snow White and the Seven Dwarfs, the journeys of little Heidi or the mysterious Aladdin and his magic lamp brightened the end of my afternoons. Nothing was better than a good story, after a whole day of penmanship and arithmetic, to appease my anxiety.

The unexpected discovery of the other Aden's notebooks came at a good time, as I was already enjoying the real stories told by Grandma Cochise. As if by chance, everything was coming together to turn me into a lover of fascinating, fabulous stories: first my grandmother, then the teacher, and now old Aden, out of the past. Mind you, my great-uncle's notebooks were smothering under the dust in an old closet and only needed the hand that would wake them from their sleep. That hand was mine. Deciphering them took me a great deal of time. That, too, was soothing.

Devastated by the sorrow she felt at my little sister's death, my mother no longer spoke, no longer ate, didn't even wash. In fact, she never left her bed. At this pace, she was in danger of sliding down the slope that had led Askar to the bottom of the hole. Because he had lost his whole family in a fire, this senior official had gone down the deep end. The fire was no accident: Askar had become pro-independence and some high-ranking Gaullist had chosen to nip Askar's ideals in the bud.

Mama was letting herself go, but Grandma did not suffer in the throes of affliction. As for me, I was discovering the life of that uncle unlike any other. According to the adults in my family, I was not gifted for real life.

'The kid's off to a bad start!' I heard their thoughts before they crossed the threshold of their lips, but they couldn't guess that. I was supposed to suffer from a vicious illness, hidden in my body, which was thinner than the stock of a vine. From an inability to adjust to the world of adults with its many traps— that's what they really thought!

As I deciphered the capricious handwriting of old Aden, I was struck by several scenes drawn by a talented hand. In each one of his drawings, one motif kept coming back: a little white boy in a blue coat holding in his hand a stick with a golden star at the end of it. Around him, brown-skinned people in old-style dress; that is, frayed clothes that must have been white in another era. In the middle of them all, a lean man with flashing eyes whose extraordinary life I would later discover. This was the Little Prince. That little boy in a blue coat, I made him mine so fast I could guess his gestures and finish his sentences before he could. That child resembled me in various ways, that's what I had decided. Béa, I knew that child better than my own parents. That child was me. I can see myself again, swimming between the banks of time. I can see myself going through the notebooks with illegible scrawls left by old Aden. In the depths of my being, I felt all the emotions of that child who wanted to fly like the birds of the savannah. I, too, wanted to fly.

My strongest wish at the time: to throw myself off the top of a cliff.

To spread out my emaciated arms, which would immediately turn into vigorously flapping wings.

To fly, to fly,

To fly and keep flying.

Years later, I realized the notebook came from an illustrated edition for little nomads who wanted to learn the secrets of the alphabet. It was distributed by a religious congregation that wanted to lead the people of the bush back onto the straight and narrow path. One of the episodes stayed with me for a long time. Let me point out, my dear child, that I could read quite properly then. In that episode, I met a boy in a blue suit who reminded me of another story I had read almost at the same time. In the second story, the little boy was perched on a tree and was looking around for another man with flashing eyes.

That man was Christ!

Something in his posture had touched me so much that I projected myself into him the way your shadow and mine come together sometimes, Béa, when we walk to the Italian grocery on Rue du Faubourg-Saint-Denis where we buy our gnocchi *napoletani* and mozzarella *di buffala*. As a child, I saw myself sitting next to Christ. You told me that Christ made a strong impression on you, too. His body, so thin, and his wounds, touched you right away. 'Why were they mean to him?' you asked more than once. I didn't know how to answer you. Your mother didn't much like me to tell you about Christ or take you to Saint-Laurent, one of the oldest churches in Paris.

As a child, I thought Christ was my contemporary. I saw myself thrown like him into the midst of those Jews with emaciated faces and eyes burning with fever. From that day on and until middle school, those mysterious scrawls and drawings were my constant companions. I preferred the freshness of those drawings to the annoying questions of my mother or Aunt Dayibo who never had a child, despite the many assaults of her old husband. I really think I understood then that tales like *The Little Prince* or the Gospel were not stories from the past, stories of people hidden behind the dark curtain of the past. I knew that these stories were accounts of our own lives. And that one day or other, we might all go through the experience of Zacchaeus, the man who was perched on a tree to see Jesus arriving in Jericho, Béa. Blue coat or not, he wasn't a boy as I thought for a while, but a very short man. A sinner. A man everyone hated and yet, not someone in need. The day I managed to penetrate the secret of his name, I was filled with joy. He was called Zacchaeus. I easily avoided the spelling trap—two c's. So, Zacchaeus is pronounced Za-cay-us. I think Johnny and his gang of tramps would have fallen into that trap, Béa. Surely Madame Annick would have been proud if she'd known of my exploit!

As I leafed through the pages over and over again, I began to absorb the biblical episode. It said Zacchaeus had amassed a lot of money and he was the chief tax collector. He was perched on his sycamore and when Jesus spoke directly to him, that rich Zacchaeus was the quickest to answer his call.

'Zacchaeus, come down fast: I must stay at your house today.'

No sooner said than done. Zacchaeus climbed down and welcomed Jesus with great joy. The important people they called Pharisees got angry. They were immensely jealous. Their wrath was boundless.

He went to stay at a sinner's house, can you imagine?

But Zacchaeus went through a rapid transformation. He overcame his fear of others. He gave himself up unhesitatingly. Would I, too, be capable of doing this one day? Listen to him, Béa:

'Look, Lord! Here and now, I give half of my possessions to the poor, and if I have cheated anybody out of anything, I will pay back four times the amount.'

And Jesus' eyes lit up:

'Today salvation has come to this house, because this man, too, is a son of Abraham.'

In my old uncle Aden's notebook, you can read that in truth, the Son of Man came to seek and to save what was lost. I instantly fell under the charm of that expression, *le Fils de l'homme*, the Son of Man, which I heard for the first time. You won't believe me, Béa, but I noticed the capital F in *Fils* right away.

The story of that man named Zacchaeus served me as a compass for many years. I'm grateful to my great-uncle who restored that biblical episode in his diaries. If Jesus was able to save a man with just one word, he could save me, too, when I find myself in a dangerous situation, like being forced to confront Johnny's gang in the schoolyard. Then I understood why grownups began to pray as soon as they felt a danger hovering over their shoulders or the shoulders of their loved ones. And I was beginning to tell myself that I'd do the same thing tomorrow if Johnny and his little soldiers were hounding me. I prayed to the Lord and Satan for that band to be annihilated by the fire of the Burning Bush that burns without ever being consumed or by the crickets who devour all the grass on the hills of Judea.

Old uncle Aden was not the only one to love Quranic and biblical stories. In our big nomadic family, everyone knew by heart the exploits of the prophets Ibrahim, Moussa and Issa, called in the Gospels Abraham, Moses and Jesus. My Aunt Dayibo told the story of the lives of saints and took the valiant Issa for a member of the family. For a long time, I believed he, too, was a child of the Château-d'Eau neighbourhood like me and my father Amine.

However, my Aunt Dayibo was the most fervent follower of the marvels and miracles reproduced in religious books. As I said before, she didn't know how to read but she knew by heart the Quranic verses and the main stages in the Prophet Mohammed's life the life of his wife Aisha. Beads in hand, Aunt

Dayibo prayed all the time. As Providence did not give her the gift of childbirth, I thought it was easier for her to identify with the venerable Aisha. Her prayer beads in hand, Aunt Dayibo prayed all the time. Her face remained inscrutable and only her triple chin and her mouth moved, mechanically. At any time of the day or night, you could catch prayers and invocations on her lips. And the hand of Fatima hanging at her neck would bounce at the end of each prayer, just in the perimeter of fat between her triple chin and her heaving breast. The poor necklace must have been worn out by the end of the day from hearing her ceaselessly pray and moan. Hanging on my aunt's neck was no sinecure. Aunt Dayibo always seemed on the verge of tears when she was stringing together praises and rounds of beads. Every morning, always on her knees, she begged Saints Aisha and Fatima to grant her a quiet day. I mean, she didn't say it like that but spoke instead of 'seeking their grace' or 'mercy.' At the end of her prayer, she would sigh that someday the 'heavenly reward' would come. When she happened to finally take me in her arms, Aunt Dayibo still did not stop mumbling. Prayer gave her the courage to face anything; she fed on it as I fed on milk and white rice.

But there was something else that bothered me. I could feel in my whole body that my presence was interrupting the continuous dialogue she had with Saint Aisha. And I knew she didn't like me very much and I probably was not part of her Kingdom of God whose colours she described with many details. Even when she talked about me, she would address her favourite saint:

'Holy Mother, Venerable Aisha, let this child regain his health.' I would pretend I didn't hear. I cried so I wouldn't hear more.

'He was born dying. It is surely an indication.'

'But only You, Saint Aisha, can come to his assistance!'

I would cry even more loudly.

'With his fledgling, baby bird of a body, he'll never go far!'

My mother was now fully recovered. She was fussing over my snotty-nosed little brother who seemed to fulfil her completely in return. Ossobleh drank his bottle like a very thirsty dromedary, hopped around in my mother's arms and then gave out two belches and three smelly farts before falling asleep immediately. His stool was yellowish, soft and stinky, which is a good sign, Béa, even if you probably don't know it, since at nine, you hold your nose when you go to the bathroom. My younger brother just smiled at everybody and never failed to burst out laughing when someone tickled his belly. He was growing very fast, to the great joy of his mother, who examined his legs, arms, muscles and reflexes every hour of the day. In short, a delightful little baby and the absolute opposite of me.

My mother no longer took care of me. Following in my mother's footsteps, Papa Beanpole ignored me too and Grandma Cochise kept the key of her silence to herself. Only Aunt Dayibo brought up the state of my health when she prayed ostentatiously, no doubt to attract the favours of Saint Aisha. She would make the seed of her husband sprout, assuming he finally managed, just once, as if by magic, to deposit that seed in her belly. One go is enough, as in poker. At least that's what the adults whispered among themselves, thinking I couldn't hear their little secrets. They didn't know I was eavesdropping behind doors. And that I rummaged through Grandma Cochise's trunks and observed everything because I've been curious, always, about everything.

And then one day there was a renewal of interest for me, or more exactly, for my foreskin. It was Grandma Cochise who put the topic on the table. I could feel that my mother was not comfortable with it. She tried to avoid the issue but that was not the best technique to get an idea out of our stubborn grandmother's head. Her reaction was extremely prompt.

'We must set a date. I'm going to tell Omar the butcher.'

At these words, my heart jumped out of its thoracic cage, my legs quivered and my head began to buzz like a swarm of hungry bees. I uttered a heartrending cry. Grandma looked daggers at me. To keep crying would only worsen my case. To stop crying wouldn't help, either. A part of my body was shaking despite my efforts to calm down. My trembling chin might set off my grandma's wrath. I had nightmares all night long: little men with huge syringes were cutting me into a thousand pieces. Led by old Omar, they had meat hooks and butcher knives. That night, I flooded my bed like never before. I always had a fragile bladder: I was used to finding a pee stain on my bed the size of an Ethiopian biscuit but the stain that morning broke the record. You would have thought it was the result of a week's work with a foreman looking over my shoulder to decide if he was happy with my production and keep me working on his site.

Grandma Cochise was putting the final touches on the organization of the ceremony. That morning, my mother didn't notice anything on my sheet. Or rather, she chose to ignore the disaster, as her attention was captured by the lucky little bum who, as soon as I came across his crooked gaze, gave me a strong urge to crap. A half hour later, Grandma Cochise was filled in by my mother or by Aunt Dayibo. Or by the little maid, I can't remember who anymore. The result of this was that Grandma hastened the moment of the operation without anaesthetic and sent Ladane to the old butcher. My impurity had lasted way too long, she proclaimed. It was high time to end it!

I absolutely didn't care for their purity, Béa.

I would have preferred to keep, as long as possible, my bit of flesh they called by weird names.

They spoke of my 'veil,'
my 'shell,'

my 'peel,'
my filth.

They had adopted the ridiculous terms of the butcher, who sometimes played barber on Saturdays. Going through his hands was not something I would enjoy later.

Nor tomorrow,
nor the day after,
nor another day of the year.

I was still a little child, Béa! How old was I? Hardly nine—okay, nine and a bit but Madame Annick would have said bits don't count for us human beings. The butcher could still wait one or two years before sharpening his blade under my nose or more exactly between my legs, that's what I was thinking. But apparently, nobody shared my opinion.

When he cut my willy, the old butcher took off a big piece because I had cried a lot, and gave it to his cat, Pompidou. Maybe my mother cried next to me, too, after entrusting my roommate to Ladane. To teach me a good lesson, old Omar had been intransigent.

Idriss, my cousin who lived at the corner of Avenue du Général-de-Gaulle and Rue des Mouchards, wasn't going to contradict me about the existence of the fat cat named after the former president of France and our TFAI. Pompidou was supposed to have a weakness for foreskins seasoned with olive oil. Idriss wasn't a real cousin, I mean, with same uncle same auntie, but that didn't matter. My mother had told me he was my cousin, that's all. Idriss had undergone the ordeal of old Omar's knife many years ago. He would be by my side like my mother, if, however, she could decide to forget the little king and his bottle for a moment. Idriss would be there to give me some useful advice. Like a coach out in the field keeping up the players' morale, he would kneel and put his hand on my shoulder while the blade was severing—zzzziiifff—that little piece of flesh, so impure in the eyes of the narrow-minded adults. I would be glad to welcome Idriss even if I hadn't been very nice to him in the past. I didn't like Idriss' fat belly or his fat thighs, and still less, his smell of garlic. As soon as he opened his mouth, garlic jumped out at you, Béa, and its shadow enveloped you. His good mother said that garlic heals everything. Headaches, chills, even tears and nocturnal pollutions. I didn't agree. When Idriss opened his mouth and garlic jumped on me, my eyes started to cry all by themselves. I wouldn't call that a medicine but a product as dangerous as Johnny and his gang of cutthroats.

Idriss wasn't the only one who carted around the stench of garlic and fried oil. His whole family carried the stench with them. His mother, called 'Mama Peugeot' by the whole neighbourhood, or, in our language, Ina Peugeot, sold fritters, paper cones full of peanuts and soft-boiled eggs in front of our schoolyard. She already smelled bad when she got there in the morning with her pots and bundles. At noon, she almost didn't smell, for the dust and scents of diesel oil had driven away the stale odours of garlic and fried oil. But no denying it, Ina Peugeot was very nice. She liked to laugh, clapping her plump hands on her fat thighs when she shared a funny story with us. She worked constantly from morning to night until the last pupil had left and Monsieur Dini, better known by the name Rubberband, had closed the gate of the Château d'Eau school behind us. Only then did Ina Peugeot break camp, but wait: she wasn't done with working like a mule. She still had to walk the two kilometres that separated our school from the Place des Chameaux, which never slept.

That's where they had the cattle market. Some people came to sell a sheep, a goat, a cow and, at holiday times, an old dromedary. Others came to buy a ewe, a billy-goat, a calf and on holidays, an old dromedary. Ina Peugeot didn't return home until late in the night. Idriss, his brothers and sisters helped her on Place des Chameaux when they weren't playing hide-and-seek near the fountain. Sometimes they would slip between the legs of the dromedaries or the cows and go to sleep in the soothing warmth of these animals. Idriss had told me that in the depths of the night there was no better hiding place. The cows were always chewing on something and the child hidden under their belly had plenty of time to observe their jaws ceaselessly opening and closing. If you were hidden there, Béa, you had to watch out for the noise that rose from the cow's stomach because she could send you a thick stream of warm poop that smelled terrible and stuck to your skin like candle wax. It happened more than once to Idriss Garlic-Face. In addition to his usual perfume, the poor guy felt warm, sticky poop dripping down his head. He made me believe it smelled exactly like freshly cut grass.

He was lying of course, because everyone knows the city cows chew on cartons and leftovers found in garbage cans. They've forgotten the flavour of the branches and leaves in the bush. Hoping that the poop from today's cows smells of fresh-cut grass is like hoping to bring down a star from the sky. What do you expect? The cows in the bush and the cows in the capital don't plod over the same red laterite earth. They're not part of the same surroundings, their sky is not the same. It's truly truly true, as you would say, that on some nights, the sky shows images printed on its sparkling body. But those images are so far away that no one really knows what they're made of. Our nomadic ancestors didn't know if they were made of terra cotta, brick or cast iron. Me, a child of the Château-d'Eau, I didn't have the faintest idea. One day, perhaps, something will trigger off in my mind.

And yet, on nights when it was very dark, I couldn't help staring at the landscape, the sky and the moon. A legend Grandma Cochise told when her eyesight was better and she was merrier spoke of the Moon in a totally magical way.

Idriss did a good job as coach. Old Omar did his. My mother was not at my side during the ordeal. She must have been wiping the butt of the little jerk who drank his bottles and slept at night the way he was supposed to. My convalescence lasted the time necessary. Over a week with a minimum of water and food. I could only count on myself to face the insults and punches that were waiting for me outside. I could only count on my obstinacy to protect my territory inside the family. It hadn't been easy to give over my body, or more exactly, my penis, to the hands of old Omar. There was no one to console me. In the past, I hadn't been very nice to my rare allies. I had been unfair to Moussa! And I wasn't very nice to Idriss either. Our relationship had broken off from the day I called him Idriss Garlic-Face. And now he'd come on his own volition to give me advice before the circumcision. At the start, I was slightly ashamed. But I didn't dare open up to him. I kept that shame to myself like a pathetic little secret to keep in my heart. Now it was time to make up for it. Outside, I had lots of enemies. Here at home, it was no better. So I needed allies at school and in our neighbourhood.

I didn't have a chance to thank Idriss the next day. He had helped me face up to the blade of the old butcher turned barber on Saturdays – and even Friday mornings for the papas who wanted their moustache trimmed so they would look important and elegant before the great Friday prayer.

Thin as a scarecrow, pale as a ghost, I couldn't sleep a wink on the days that followed my circumcision. The people around me considered me a man from now on, so I was supposed to stop complaining once and for all. The more they scolded me, the more I shrank into myself.

'Act like a man, Aden!'

During the day, I remained stretched out next to Grandma Cochise. At the end of the afternoon, they'd take me back to the house. In both cases, stretched out and feverish, only my eyes moved, only my ears heard and registered everything. I had the impression that my hearing was sharper than my sight. From afar, I could hear the sound of a match struck by someone smoking on the corner of the street. Grandma Cochise couldn't see well, but a whole bunch of seconds ahead, I could inform her that Ina Peugeot would drop by to say hello. I could guess the heavy step of Idriss Garlic-Face's mother before my eye fell upon her obese body. My spirit would wander while my body remained in the grip of fever.

When night fell over my neighbourhood, a few lights remained on in front of the houses of the richest among us. Stretched out on my mat, I would listen to the sound of the night. Madame Annick might have said Djibouti was turning into a phantom city. I was intoxicated by nocturnal sounds as I waited for my wound to scar over.

Farewell, my foreskin!

Farewell, my childhood!

I'm no longer a kid.

Something began to move in my crotch.

I changed.

The little restaurants on Greasy Spoon Street would be packed when it was dark. They said foreign women got into these little restaurants right near us. They would order a beer and open it with their teeth. Then, with their legs spread, they chatted among themselves while waiting for the boldest men. Some customers would come over to them, then laugh with them before becoming their men for the night. Those women with scarlet lips in quest of darlings knew how to wait. Late into the night, their laughs could be heard all the way to the depths of my neighbourhood. Men, drunk with fatigue collapsed under the tables between the open legs. Between two bursts of diabolical laughter, the women would reach orgasm. I learned this word much later. I wondered how the drunks managed to bite the fat of their thighs. Were these women putting on an act? I never met these men, nor these women, but everyone in our neighbourhood knew of their exploits.

The first time Aunt Dayibo caught Ladane the maid telling these stories she summoned Saint Aisha to come in person and save those 'poor wretches' and their rascally customers. Grandma Cochise supposedly scolded Ladane the maid for having reported the gossip here and there around our house. Her daughter, Aunt Dayibo, the younger sister of my dad Amine, greatly enjoyed the maid's stories but in secret. She invoked all the saints who populated Heaven, male and female, but she always listened to the dirty stories to the very end. Everything sounded true to Aunt Dayibo as long as the voice of the person telling the story was captivating. Aunt Dayibo's heart accepted Ladane the maid's stories as it accepted that the earth was created in seven days and seven nights.

As for me, I saw things differently. I only thought things true as long as that was useful to me. I shared Aunt Dayibo's fascination for the stories about creation that are spelled out in the Quran, as well as those that told us what happened to the Prophet Issa, whom Madame Annick called Jesus the Christ! Speaking of the Prophet, everything was faithfully recorded, claimed Aunt Dayibo, who was as round as the Queen of Hearts in *Alice in Wonderland*. Everything, from the day of his birth to his death at the age of thirty-three. My father Amine had gone beyond that age, but no one would preserve his memory with the same ardour as the memory of Christ.

When I was a little older and Madame Annick or a new teacher asked us to tell a story—they called that a composition, Béa, and you'll be great at that exercise, too, in two or three years—I would slip in one or two adventures that happened to my father and I'd mix in some of Ladane the maid's stories, or old Uncle Aden's, or even the stories of Grandma Cochise when she was a little shepherd watching over her goats. Mind you, Grandma Cochise did not like to be reminded of her age. She came from another world and another time. As a child, she had heard of the French, English and Italian domination. All three of them had divided and shared the land of our ancestors between them. That was before the TFAI! At that time, the time of General de Gaulle, the brain of a dreamy High Commissioner hatched a name for our land that was easier to retain.

Three little letters.

CFS.

Côte française des Somalis.

That morning, it all began in an ordinary way—and this at a time, Béa, when I did not yet dance when I walked. It must have been a banal morning. In the country of childhood and family warmth, there were no extraordinary events to report from the previous days. On the preceding mornings, the sun had left its cotton wool bed and gone up to the sky to drive away ominous looking clouds. I think—no, I know now—that my life was turned upside down that morning. And that lightning struck my frail shoulders. My mother told me later that the sky was clear, surprisingly clear, but how could she be sure? What is certain is that I got up early that morning. And I waited for my mother on the edge of the bed. I waited for her a long time. Then she came in, without saying a word. She dressed me, as usual, in the shadowy light of the room. Always silent. Sour-tempered and distant. Not the ghost of a smile, not a kiss.

I can see myself again on the street, just across from our house.

Everything in slow motion, frozen in the present tense of trauma.

My mother pulls me by the hand.

I fall.

My shorts bite the dust.

She throws hard words in my face, pulls me again.

I fall again and my shorts bite the dust.

She stops, catches her breath and pulls me once again.

She wrenches me so hard I feel my collarbone dislocating.

And I fall again, this time worse than before.

It hurts but I don't say anything. No word comes out of my mouth.

My mother pulls me again.

And I fall.

It's Grandma Cochise who puts an end to the ordeal.
She's been sitting in her usual spot since sunrise.
In a firm voice, she scolds my mother:
'Don't you see that child can't walk?'
I turn to my grandmother.
My mother pulls me by the arm once more and I fall like all the other times.
My mother finally lets go of my hand, breathless.
She takes a few steps before sitting down to catch her breath.
I stay there with my butt in the dust.
It's the longest moment of my life.
Its weight is the heaviest.
My mother finally opens her mouth to piece things together.
'Why is he falling today?'
The calm, clear voice of Grandma Cochise comes forth:
'His leg doesn't hold.'
In a panic, my mother pounces on me, picks me up and wipes the dust off my shorts.
Her eyes soften.
She massages my leg.
I think I can't feel anything.
The ache is elsewhere.
It has migrated to my head.
It's a corset.
I will wear it all my life.
There's a crowd in the house. The passers-by stop to glean fragments of information. The neighbours come and go, some more worried than others. The matrons comfort my mother as if she had just lost a small child. I'm passed from hand to hand like when I was an infant and all I did was cry. They pick me up, weigh me in their hands. They squeeze my upper limbs, my torso, my spine. They massage my legs, rub me down with pomades. I think I don't feel much of anything. My face is mournful, my eyes round and wet. It doesn't particularly hurt, or at least I have no memory of pain, it's not even smarting. They schlep me from clinic to clinic. The nurses uncork flasks

of alcohol and lay out rolls of cotton. They glance at my leg. No wound to be cleaned. Their surprise was on their lips:

'Madame, we can't do anything for him.'

When they saw us again a week later, there was no surprise anymore, but a definitive reproach.

'Madame, go see a real doctor...'

I think that after the circumcision, the beginning of the end of childhood dated from that visit to the first real doctor who saw us at the Peltier hospital, the biggest in the country. Doctor Toussaint was a real Frenchman from France like Madame Annick. He wore a white smock that hid everything except the tips of his brown shoes. When I heard his steps coming, making the floor shake a little, I instinctively knew that Doctor Toussaint had solid legs, nicely rounded in his socks, and the robust body of a soldier. After he had exchanged a few words with the nurse, she translated into French what Mama had said. Doctor Toussaint finally turned toward me with a grave face. He looked me up and down and then picked me up. When I was in his arms, I felt like a little bird floating in the palm of his hand.

A second nurse came in with a big blue bucket. As she set it down in the middle of the office, she spilled a few drops of water on the floor. Hanging in the air, I huddled up out of fear of what was going to happen in the minutes to come. I had no time to read anything at all on Mama's face. A surprise was waiting for me. Doctor Toussaint's green eyes continued to feel me out. And now, he squatted down with his butt on his heels, and in this position, he was still much taller than I was. With a sharp pull, he got my legs out of my shorts, grey with dust from my multiple falls. Then he picked me up. My little body was floating between his two solid arms. Then he looked me up and down once more and dunked me into the big blue basin. He was intent on having me sit down in the water, Béa. What a strange idea! my mother must have thought. And yes, he was trying to make me stand up on my two legs and make me sit down again before straightening up my body.

All this time, my mother hadn't said a single word. She was watching Doctor Toussaint's big, hairy hands kneading my whole body from head to toe. She had never seen a doctor treat me like that. And this time it wasn't the neighbourhood clinic. We were at the Peltier hospital. A real doctor was talking with my mother Zahra. She did not understand the language of Madame Annick, but a little nurse had done a good job translating her words for Doctor Toussaint. My mother kept a solemn silence. Alone on a desert island surrounded by bull sharks, she would have been more talkative than she was in front of this doctor scrutinising her with the blade of his eyes, as green and luminous as sapphire.

My mother thought he wanted to get something out of her. If someone had asked a precise question, she would have confessed that she knew nothing of the illness that had been eating away at me for the last few days. One morning I got up in this state. Would her words be taken at face value? If someone had wanted to probe further, she would have added that she'd been the last one to realize that a strange, unknown force kept pulling me down. She tried desperately to pull me up. The result was always the same: I would fall down again and remain with my butt in the dust. With Doctor Toussaint, she was more talkative. She said it was the grandmother who'd pinpointed where the problem was: my right leg. It was my right leg that gave way every time she tried to pull me as she did every day, for she had a thousand things to do in the morning and no time to give in to my whims. And because I still was a dreamy, lazy child, she was only doing me a favour by shaking me that way. She would have revealed all that, if only Doctor Toussaint had asked her to say more about that particular day and the problem that brought us to ask for his services three days later.

Doctor Toussaint remained utterly insensitive to the flow of thoughts that were rushing through Mama's head. He continued to squeeze my arms, my legs and even the bones of my skull. I could hear his slow, calm breathing. I was a little bird in his hands. An object of study. An enigma.

Thanks to the caresses and nice words the family lavished on me, I found a bit of comfort. My leg hurt less but I knew I wasn't out of the woods. I didn't know if my leg would take long to heal and I was preparing myself in my own way, trying to escape by every possible means. I spent whole days sitting almost motionless, getting used to watching the people and things around me. As the grandson of nomads, I would dream of pets. Imagining had a soothing effect on my heart. I imagined stroking a ram's neck, sliding my hand along his horns, driving away the flies buzzing around his eyes. Sometimes I saw myself as a sulky goat and sometimes as a bleating lamb, indifferent to the gaze of adults. I would also take refuge in the past. The time machine had no secrets for me anymore; I took it apart and put it back together like a mechanic removing a part of a car, cleaning it and putting it right back under the hood.

This daydream had many charms. It wound along like a river whose source was in childhood. All I had to do, Béa, was close my eyes to recover all those images and sensations. The ballet of ants in the yard of my elementary school and its half blue, half white gate was another of my favourite distractions. I would also watch the long trail of ash that began in our kitchen and then slipped under the clay pots and jars and aluminium saucepans to go lose itself at the neighbours'. And those ants—what a ballet and what a landscape! Watching ants isn't as easy as you may think, dear girl. You need a lot of time and to make sure the noise of the city doesn't contaminate you.

I had all the time in the world. Now, the other children who were no longer my friends played endless games of soccer on vacant lots. Only the ants kept me company. They were there for me, like the geckos. Ever faithful, even at night.

One day, my mother decided to take me to Siesta Beach. I was sad to leave my ants. Aunt Dayibo came along. Once they reached the deserted beach, they got into a long conversation about marriage, dowry and baptism. There were no ants on the beach. And it was better that way because otherwise the wind from the city would have carried them away and thrown them into the sea that was beginning to lash the rocks.

I felt alone.

Without my ants.

Without my geckos.

Alone, once again.

I tried hard to find some kind of distraction but I could see no other recourse than my mother.

I threw a little stone at the women to attract their attention. They kept on talking. A minute later, I threw another little stone that got my mother to react. She finally realised what I was up to.

Me (facing her): 'Mama, can you put me in the water? I want to go in, I've had my leg in the sand for the last hour and I'm tired of it!'

Her (back turned): 'The doctor said sand is good for your leg.'

In the neighbourhood, tongues started wagging rather quickly. The most indelicate people felt sorry for my mother, my father, and the whole household. The foolhardy pointed at Grandma, murmuring that the family was just reaping what the matron had sowed for all those years. But the worst of it was, the boldest were saying indignantly, that she put the blame on a poor child who had offended neither the Lord nor Satan. The wildest imaginations claimed that good Doctor Toussaint was going to send me off to France for surgery because he'd taken my case to heart. After a few weeks, the French doctors would take off the pin and the nails. Then I'd do my rehab in a specialised centre. When I got back, I'd have to wear an orthopaedic shoe and all I'd have to do was shine it every day because it had to keep its nice, black colour.

After the sarcasm and insinuations of the adults, things took another turn. I was subjected to the insults of their children even more than before. I moaned under their blows. I ran away, hopping on one leg when some little punk, often the weakest and quietest of the gang, decided to take me for a target. Stones rained down on my head. I had only one escape: to flee, far away. To flee, even on my one good leg.

They rained stones on me less frequently, for sure, than they punched me in the face or belly. Less frequently than they spat in my face. But every day, I was insulted and cursed. Put all that end to end and you get a despicable chain.

'With his leg, he won't be able to run after the goats like his nomad ancestors.'

'Hey, you, you better be good at school!'

'With that build, you won't even make it as a docker at the port.'

'See his leg? It looks like a corkscrew!'

'You'll never score on a penalty kick with that club foot.'

'Look at that old man's leg, all dried up and twisted. It's the only one like that in the world!'

Memories of the clinic were further and further away and Doctor Toussaint's recommendations had sunk into oblivion. Ossobleh was the new king of the household. I secretly hated the whole family but I kept my thoughts to myself. Besides, nobody ever thought of asking my opinion about anything. Nobody cared about me. I was growing up at my own bizarre pace. Nobody was waiting for me. I made plans in my head, Béa: run and catch this world that eluded me. Leave the confines of this narrow world forever.

You know, Béa, every time I think back to this episode it tears me apart. It tears at me because I'm forced to dive back into what I lived through from that terrible morning on. Memories pour in from all over. Memory is an imperious force, a current that carries everything away in its path. Impossible to control, impossible to escape from. At this very moment, it makes me relive what I saw and experienced then, and my heart bleeds and I'm soaked in sweat. You asked why I dance when I walk. Now you know why. It all began that morning in the dust of the family courtyard. How old was I, Béa? Seven or eight, your age yesterday. And if that past can seem far off to us, memory takes me back there again. And 'far off' suddenly becomes so near. Ever since that ordeal, I am the same and I am someone else, my sweet little Béa.

Someone else, yes.

Someone who dances every day.

Someone who dances without wanting to.

Someone who dances when he walks.

I trotted along behind Ladane so often I was forgetting the charm of school. I was neglecting reading, which is, in a way, a conversation with ghosts called characters. No need to be a genius to realize Ladane was no ghost. Her face, her pouting lips, her clumsy hairdo—it all contributed to turn my heart upside down. Now, I don't turn up my nose at reading and like me, Béa, you love reading. But not everybody shared this taste for reading in my neighbourhood. Watch out, you'll go blind, my mother Zahra would warn me, prey to a new terrifying fear when she saw me devouring *Pif le Chien* or an issue of *Picsou Magazine*, my favourite comics. That passion for reading brought me closer to girls who intimidated me a lot. A passion that came with a price, too. Since I loved reading more than anything and since two or three girls shared that vice with me, I was the object of mockery from the boys.

'Hey faggot, come on, try running!'

I was jeered at often.

Mocked a hundred times.

I even received some angry kicks.

I endured vulgar insults:

'Get the hell out of here, you faggot!'

I hastened my step.

The shouts and laughter intensified:

'Watch out, you're gonna collapse!'

With my book or my magazine under my arm, I tried to run to avoid their persecution. One morning, some of these morons pursued me with carnivorous snarls. I could feel their breath on my neck. I trotted on, looking around for an adult. By chance, there was a gathering of women not too far off. I was saved, this time. I'd only ventured this far out of my neighbourhood to borrow a magazine from some girls who passed them along when they'd finished reading them. They knew I read everything that fell into my hands. I didn't even turn down my nose at photo novellas. Books, journals, magazines and comics were such rare commodities in our neighbourhood that I was always ready to brave the intense heat and the jeers to go get an old book falling to pieces or a waterlogged copy of *Paris Match* at the other end of the city.

Another time, I had boldly limped out so far from home that I got lost in a forest of little wooden houses and anonymous streets. I was walking around in circles and as luck would have it, I had just gone through a rocky alley again. Seeing me wandering, an imbecile in khaki shorts got up and walked toward me. Suddenly, he grabbed a bottle and threw it in my face. The bottle crashed a few inches from my head. It almost left me with one eye.

'You dirty fag! Next time, I won't miss your ass!'

This incident cooled my ardour for a while, Béa. As days went by, my reserve of books and journals melted like raindrops on the dried-out plain of Yoboki. I absolutely needed to venture out again even with fear in my guts. I had to quench my thirst for reading, stay alert and send my neurons into a panic. I read anything that fell into my hands, for I still had a lively appetite. The labels on cans of food and cartons could not escape my probing eye. Everything that had miraculously landed in our slum—sooner or later, I would find it. Comic books all ripped up? Yes. The fine novels Madame Annick mentioned with such delight? No. I had never seen *The Mysteries of Paris, Letters from my Mill, The Three Musketeers, Les Misérables, Little What's-His-Name, Nobody's Boy* or *Alone in the World* lying around in my neighbourhood. Things that happened in school never managed to reach our households. Conversely, the smells and awful din of our neighbourhood never got through the gates of the school. Only the children went from the neighbourhood to the school in the morning, then came back at the end of the afternoon. When I returned home after school, I would sometimes recite a poem or sing a song Madame Annick had first read or sang to us and asked us to underline the hard words she explained afterwards. When I came home with part of a poem or story in my mouth, things would go on with no problem. I would begin singing *'Sur le pont d'Avignon'* to Ladane the maid, who listened to me to the end, her light brown eyes fixed on mine. Mama would bail out after two lines and Grandma Cochise would scold me before I even opened my mouth.

But Ladane listened to me to the very end. She'd ask, with her look of a little puppy, what my song was about. I'd tell her what I had retained from Madame Annick's explanations. I repeated that the French-from-France were happy people who dance all night in the moonlight. She'd be surprised and ask if it was like that all the time. No, not all the time, but very often, I ventured. And what's that, Davignon? I'd sigh and invent a story, trying to hide my embarrassment with a laugh. Then I'd take back what I had said and pompously added: 'Well, that's easy. It's a bridge, it's a bridge! All you have to do is listen to the song, Ladane. There's the Eiffel Tower'—that, she remembers because she'd seen it on a postcard—'but there's also the bridge, *Le pont Davignon*', the Davignon Bridge. I recited the big cities of France like Paris the capital with its thousand lights, like Marseille from where we get the wonderful soap that washes better than all the soaps of all our families taken together. Like Toulon with lots of soldiers and military boats, too. I didn't know yet what city Madame Annick was from, but it didn't matter much to me anymore.

Ladane came to us during the rainy season toward the end of my time in elementary school. I fell in love with her as soon as I saw her. I hung around her like a dog looking for his master. I watched her on the sly. The naughty girl was well aware of it when she pulled up part of her dress and my gaze managed to slip inside her thighs, which were muscular from walking. She had no cause to be envious of the French high school girls who strutted around in bathing suits on Triton Beach and shrieked with joy as they came out of the water, twisting their hair like mermaids, to wring it out. None of them equalled the charm and mystery of Lois Lane in the vigorous arms of Superman. *My* Lois Lane—you guessed it—was Ladane. She had a certain rustic beauty. She smelled of cooking oil and detergent. Her smell intoxicated me as soon as she drew near. When she did the dishes, I admired the tip of her long fingers in the soapy water. When she bent down to put the dishes away, I swept my eyes over her back, her calves, but above all her buttocks.

Tall, thin but supple, Ladane hadn't been well fed during her difficult youth. Her cheeks were hollow, even when she burst out laughing and whispered inaudible words to me. Her knees knocked together when she walked. Ladane was older than I was; I think she must have been around 17. She had never set foot in a school. She wasn't married either. Before landing at our house, she had worked for another family in another city or big village named Dasbiyu or Daouenleh, I forget. Drought had ravaged the bush where Ladane was born. Poverty had dispersed her family, throwing one member here, another further away. I was glad she'd chosen our house. Every morning, I watched her work. She got up before everybody else, even before the rooster gave out its annoying cock-a-doodle-doo.

I had just entered adolescence. Maybe you can understand me now. I don't ask you about your boyfriends and I hope you won't think I'm silly. Ladane is the flag under which I navigated the first flush of adolescence. Ladane conquered me very early. She was the lotus flower who lorded it over the mud of my neighbourhood. The little devil had a hell of a body but no strength in her arms, which were a little too long compared to the rest of it. Ladane had trouble lifting the water bucket over her shoulders. When I got up to help her, Grandma Cochise would give me an angry look. Ladane had to sweep the courtyard, do the wash, run to Hadja Khadidja's to bring back a kilo of rice, a bunch of leeks, or a can of sardines depending on the money my mother had given her. I was not to get involved in these domestic chores; that was Ladane's business. I was to concentrate on my schoolwork, Cochise thought. She had authorized me to go into Hadja Khadidja's shop, where you could find every imaginable product: from powdered cheese to barred cages for trapping mice, rats and the little snakes that are often more dangerous than big boas.

I was afraid of everything and didn't fall asleep easily. Afraid of Hadja Khadidja when she slipped her spider-like fingers into the bags of rice, flour or red beans and they came out all white, covered with starch. Hadja Khadidja would stick her forefinger and thumb into her mouth. She would lick them ostentatiously, sucking them with obvious pleasure. As soon as Ladane the maid stood before big, fat Hadja Khadidja she would stammer and break into excuses. The ogress with rings on her fingers would scold her maliciously.

Every morning, my mother put a certain sum of money into the palm of Ladane's right hand. I tried several times to guess how much but I could never tell for sure. Once or twice, I saw the crumpled bill and the two or three coins close up, but I wasn't good enough in arithmetic yet to get the sum. Madame Annick would have scolded me if she had known that I wasn't good at arithmetic now that I was in middle school. Depending on that sum, I could or could not ask for candy or drinks. I didn't care about roasted peanuts. What I wanted was to trot along behind Ladane and admire the braid that went down along her back and swung with every sway of her hips. If Ladane started to run, I could see her braid dance around and caress her back. I would drag along my rebellious leg, but my eyesight was excellent and everybody knew I had a piercing gaze.

I trotted along behind Ladane, admiring the flexible muscles of her back. She would have been a wonderful swimmer like your mother Margherita who does the crawl and breaststroke with disconcerting ease. Unlike Moussa, who sat next to me at school and hadn't talked to me for weeks, I didn't know how to swim. I would splash around in the sea but I'd never set foot in a pool. There wasn't a single pool in the native city of my childhood. Another point of difference from Moussa, I didn't like fritters or samosas. I hated eggs that dried out the inside of your mouth. When Moussa's mother gave eggs to him, I infallibly knew it, because Moussa would give off stinky belches. I held my nose and shook my head but Moussa continued to draw round letters with his brand-new pen, pretending he hadn't seen me making disgusted faces. Finally, I'd pinch my nose and Moussa kept on drawing as if nothing was the matter. Maybe he imagined I was a ghost like the ones you see in the comic strips Madame Annick read to us sometimes at the end of the day, when we had done our work well.

No doubt about it, Ladane was innocent. She came from the bush. Her parents couldn't keep her because they were either poor or dead. I did not understand how adults could make dozens of children and then let them go, or drop them here or there as if they were a cumbersome suitcase. Adults enraged me. I imagined that when they were younger, Ladane's parents were the terrorist kind, like Johnny and his gang, who sowed only violence in their path. As soon as I brought up her parents, Ladane the maid looked at me with the eyes of a frightened puppy. And yet she was not a little girl anymore. She was a desirable young woman, going on seventeen. At least that's what she told everybody: because she came from the bush and out there, in the djebels, nobody knew their real date of birth. Nobody sang a song on the day of her birth. Nobody baked a cake, like Madame Annick for her children. Nobody had notified the imam or the registry officer.

But what was I thinking, Béa? There was no mosque in the djebel. The faithful had to manage alone in their shacks, that is, holes in the mountain with no electricity or dishes. They did not have the benefit of religious knowledge to help them grow up. I knew, from Grandma Cochise, that those people all had eyes kind of close together and their eyebrows had the shape of a circumflex. They looked very stupid because every night the children would search for light in their shack which was darker than Satan's ass. Some never even wiped off the drool hanging from their lips: they were called the djebel idiots. They ended up as butchers or murderers. Luckily, Ladane had escaped the drought and famine in the djebel. Even if she had to work from cockcrow to sunset at our house, even if she ran to the corner of the courtyard that served as a kitchen to make the pots clink and give Mama the dish of white beans or chickpea soup my father loved. As soon as she heard the infernal noise of my father's moped, Ladane jumped up like a big cat and remained on duty till the end of dinner. Then she had to wash the utensils and tidy up the kitchen. If Papa Beanpole left something on his plate, she had to hand it to the matron. Grandma would remind Ladane that you must not stuff yourself with food at night because it wasn't very good for digestion except for children like Ossobleh who had to fill his belly at all hours of the day and leave nice, soft and smelly poop as proof. Grandma sniffed his poop with delight and emotion. For Ossobleh, who was going on five, she preferred his green and yellow poop to my goat turds. It wasn't my fault if I didn't like to eat, if my leg always hurt, if the visit to the doctor yielded no results and that leg filled me with shame. It wasn't my fault if Ladane had landed at our house and I loved the brown eyes of that girl from the djebel who was much older than me. In a year or two, Grandma would find her a husband—some butcher from the djebel perhaps. And me, I'd have to find a wall to hide behind, and sob and lament, sheltered from the matron's eyes.

I never saw Moussa Two-Oeils again. I nicknamed him like that because he had a god-awful time mastering complicated, irregular plural nouns in French. He was the first, but not the last, to say *chevals, animals and oeils,* instead of *chevaux, animaux, yeux* in eighth grade. Somehow, he managed to make it into middle school, Moussa Two-Oeils did. The great majority of pupils at the Château-d'Eau school went no further, Béa. Why spend more time lingering inside the jungle of the French language? Goodbye school, hello street! And if they still wanted to play and go on dreaming like children, the parents were there to set them straight. The butchers' sons were soon going to arm themselves with knives and cutlasses in their turn. The carpenters' sons were going to stick pencils inherited from their father or grandfather behind their ears, the baker's daughters were going to watch over the breadbaskets. Children whose fathers drove a bus like Moussa Two-Oeils would find themselves behind the wheel. But I remained stuck. No one cared to push me in any direction at all. I stayed the course. I had left school with my head held high. I was, as my report card said, 'admitted to pursue my studies in secondary school.' But that was not all. I had graduated 'With the congratulations of the Principal' and collected a bunch of prize books.

I never saw Moussa Two-Oeils again. At ten or eleven, he was already a big, burly guy. A big mouth, too. Strange rumours circulated about him. Some believed he was behind bars for petty thefts. Others claimed he hung out in Legionnaire bars and he'd turned into their pansy. Countless girls and boys had fallen into this trap before him. Nobody had ever seen someone come back from the swampy, reptilian world of the Legion.

One day at noon, two years earlier, I was on the big road that goes through the Château-d'Eau neighbourhood, holding my aunt Dayibo's hand. She was walking fast that day and her mind was elsewhere. I was trotting behind her and every thirty seconds she would give my hand a great yank that propelled me forward. I was on the point of collapsing every time, but my aunt's energy put me back on my feet. Or more exactly on my left foot, the valid one, while I swayed my hip like mad on the right side. It was my new habit: the rockabilly sway, as I learned ten years later. That day at noon, Aunt Dayibo wasn't sweating. She didn't have bad breath. It was one of my first walks outside. And my bad leg raised a little dust every time I swayed my hip. I measured the progress I'd made: I could walk and who knows, maybe I'd be running soon. Fly. And play soccer again with the little brats who'd kept me off the neighbourhood team that wasn't even a real team. None of the players had the right shorts, the right shirt and studded shoes. Besides, all the children hanging out on the field had the right to join. In short, it wasn't a team but a mill. Still, I envied them, from afar.

Halfway through our walk, a ballet of big trucks with canvas tops full of French Legionnaires drove by, coming from the opposite direction. I had the feeling they were staring at us. My heart was pounding, but my aunt didn't seem to be slowing down, or mind the heavy traffic. I stopped, out of breath. My aunt stopped, too, not happy at all.

'Come on, let's not stay in the middle of the sidewalk.'

I had the bright idea of asking her a question just to catch my breath. It was always like that; when my legs failed me, I had to count on my brain.

'Why are they here?'

'What do you mean?'

'Why did they come here?'

'Because they're our colonisers.'

'Our co…?'

'Because they're stronger than we are.'

At the end of my second year of middle school, the summer of 1978 began with exceptionally mild weather. Usually, at this time of year, everybody would hide as soon as the burning wind from the desert began to blow on our little houses with aluminium roofs. As early as May, the khamsin made a timid attack that rapidly grew stronger. Scorching heat clamped its lid on the city. The air quickly became stifling. Big rings appeared under armpits. You had to change your shirt quickly, take a shower. That's what my father did every noon before getting on his moped to go back to work. Me, I didn't change my shirt, Béa: I wore only low-necked T-shirts. And now, all of a sudden, thunderstorms were drumming on the roofs of the neighbourhood, forcing the chief of the family to leave her control post. Yet she was the only one who could reassure me, as my parents were preoccupied with other things. The cyclone that devastated the city came after the storms. India was to blame for the monsoon, I would learn later. Grandma's skirt was no protection against the torrential rain. The roof of the house did not resist the gusts of wind for long. They brought in an odour of rotten fish from the sea. Torrents of water were unleashed in the alleys, carrying off telegraph poles and cars. After that, they carried along tree trunks and chunks of houses ripped off their base. The wadi of Ambouli rose from its bed and sowed desolation everywhere.

I remained speechless before the spectacle of death. Swollen oxen, cows with no hoofs and sheep with no tail were roasting in the sun. But that wasn't all, Béa. The cyclone killed people, too. Often, their bodies would be found in the mangrove or in the sea. Everything poured into it. Mothers tore their faces with their nails because their children hadn't come home for three days. Then they would gather before the wadi of Ambouli or on the ruins of their former neighbourhood. They prayed with all their strength. All of them were afraid of the same thing: finding themselves looking at the corpse of their offspring, dragged in by the waters.

You should have seen how I prayed with them. Aunt Dayibo was proud of me. She told me our holy mother Aisha loved teenagers like me. I knew prayer wouldn't change how things went but prayer did transform people and they could actually change things. I didn't just pray. I had a plan to fight the cyclone. The sooner the better. Maybe as soon as next month, insha'Allah. If adults asked for my opinion, I'd tell them what to do. There certainly was a solution, and I'd found it all by myself by paying attention to the stories Grandma Cochise told me when I was manhandled by fever. You want to know my solution? It's pretty simple, Béa. All you had to do to avoid damage in the city was to cover the houses' roofs with thick tar, without forgetting the cars and tree trunks. That's what old Nouh or Noah did to waterproof the Ark. The waters of the Flood slipped over the Ark without endangering the lives of the animals swarming in its belly. The rain poured down, the rivers flowed out of their beds, the fields became lakes and the lakes turned into seas, the Ark creaked, pitched and rolled but held out. On the last day of the seventh week, it was greeted by a rainbow. Noah accomplished this exploit more than 2,000 years ago. I suggested renewing the exploit. And that's what *I* would have suggested if only the adults were willing to pay attention to me!

After a few days of panic, the deluge ended. The population's prayers had nothing to do with it. The monsoon came and went like the sirocco in Sicily, where we spend our summer vacations. Everything finally comes to an end. But as you can imagine, right after the end of the cyclone, my morale was pretty low because Ladane was very busy and I didn't have much to read. My old box of comics and books had been swept away by the waves. Impossible to get my hands on an old magazine or a *Paris Match* with the picture of imam Khomeini who'd taken over the throne of the Shah of Iran the year before. People had other, more urgent needs. No water, no electricity. No sewers and no food. Famine was threatening. Every morning, I was surprised to find myself alive. My leg hurt horribly. No medicine to dull the pain. There was only pain. There was anger. Jealousy. Resentment. I was almost fourteen and I was lonely. The other teenagers shunned me like the plague.

My leg kept me away from kids my age.

I would have liked to play soccer with them on the vacant lots.

My anger simmered inside me.

It could not express itself openly.

I was afraid of getting clouted by a kid or a parent.

That someone as incompetent as Doctor Toussaint who had his patients paddle around in a blue basin could have the title of healer made me sneer. Despite their white coats, they were incapable of treating anyone. Incapable of putting a name on the illness that was gnawing away at their bones. That Doctor Toussaint was worthless. His title was an insult to the profession. An insult to the real French-from-France. The ones I knew were good and effective like Madame Annick. That doctor couldn't be French. He was a fake Frenchman. An imposter, Béa! Maybe he was Belgian, like Hergé, the inventor of Tintin.

My parents were worthless, too, worse than the other adults. They pretended to ignore my pain when the deluge brought it back, or at least that's what I thought. Yet one day, I was flabbergasted. Never will I forget the day I surprised my father crying his eyes out. His sorrow had nothing to do with my own torments. All the adults were crying that day. And us, their children, we cried, too, just to fool them. Some parents, bearded, grown-up men and everything, sobbed so hard their glottis nearly stuck in their throat, while others sniffed noisily. My father's crying was somewhere in the middle, for he, too, loved the Egyptian president, Gamal Abdel Nasser, who'd given his name to our avenue and he had just died. The news that floored all the adults was just that: the death of General Nasser, who was unknown to me. His name had never been mentioned in history class.

And yet, they said in the neighbourhood that General Nasser had donated guns and food when our people needed it most, when French Legionnaires were massacring or deporting the people who didn't want France anymore. They wanted to liberate the TFAI. Yes, liberate the TFAI, that is, drive out the French with Egyptian rifles. They were separatists, as I learned later. The Gaullists who ruled the territory imprisoned them or deported them to France. The rest of the activists were exiled in the neighbouring country: Somalia. And now, after the ravages of the cyclone, it was Nasser who had died without warning us. That's why the adults had been crying and beating their chests for the last 24 hours to express their helplessness and their despair. So this General Nasser had been on our side. Without his support, we would have been sunk. Was the TFAI to remain the TFAI forever?

The illness that gnawed at me had a name: poliomyelitis. And an origin: Johnny tripping me up. The same Johnny who attacked the only dog in the neighbourhood. A dog that haunted my nights. When Papa Beanpole came home very late at night, the mutt would bark timidly. He was a dirty-looking mongrel, who tried to announce its presence with little yelps. He'd lie down again immediately, knowing that no one was paying any attention to him, and fall back into his old dog lethargy, dreaming of the bone waiting for him in the old metal box that served him as a bowl after the neighbourhood rooster gave out its unnerving cock-a-doodle-do. I always wondered why dogs' eyes are always thirsty. When you were little, you used to draw nice clean puppies with pretty colours. Even if you liked horses and unicorns better. When you turned six, you asked us why we didn't have a dog or a cat in the house. You knew Margherita had a Dalmatian all through her childhood. And then, what had to happen happened. Dogs do not live as long as their master or mistress. Maia's death plunged your mamma into mourning and I think she didn't want to see you go through the same experience.

No pets in the landscape of my childhood. Except for that dirty old dog. Like all his kind, he had those thirsty eyes. I felt like giving him something to drink so his eyes could become normal eyes, that certainly can cry but remain normal—not always wet and surrounded by flies, I mean. As a kid, I wanted to shout to him: 'Hey, watch out, Mr. Dog! Or else the doctors will come and give you a shot.' Eye doctors give you a shot even in the eyes and they don't care if it hurts. They tell you it's for your own good and you have to stay seated nice and straight on your behind. If you move, the needle can damage your eye. Your eye won't be thirsty anymore, it will be dead like the right eye of Askar the Madman, who doesn't know himself on what day that eye became all blank and useless.

The thirsty eyes of that old dog haunted my nights for a long time. He would drag himself along on his hindquarters. The neighbours didn't notice he was there anymore except for the band of terrorists headed by their boss, Nasty Johnny. Johnny had mounted a conspiracy against the animal. He said we should act like good Muslims: no dog deserved to live among us. The gang of terrorists went up as far as the Rimbaud neighbourhood. On the way, they would massacre wandering cats and push around the beggars gathered before the Hadji Dideh mosque. They stirred up trouble all along a route of about two or three kilometres. Then they went down to our Château-d'Eau neighbourhood to bombard the poor old dog lying in front of the shop of Hadja Khadidja, who scared me because of her long spidery fingers.

The terrorist-in-chief said he saw a story on TV showing how Muslims in Mecca kept stones hidden under their white clothes. How they go to a spot in the desert and bombard with stones the places where Satan is supposed to have passed. Once the satanic spots are covered with stones, they leave to walk around the great black stone again. There is often a lot of jostling and the oldest die, smothered. At the time, I refused to accept Johnny's version, but he was right on one point, as I learned later. How can people who've come to seek the peace of the Lord be killed by their neighbours who've also come to seek the peace of the Lord? Sometimes I tell myself that adults are completely weird. That behaviour was incomprehensible to me but I kept it to myself. I never shared this with anybody, Béa, because I'd run the risk of getting slapped so hard it would take my ears off. I preferred to stay out of trouble. I had no desire to infuriate the most narrow-minded of my uncles.

But in that pilgrimage story, some details drew my attention. The devil's in the details, right? I'll say it again, that story seemed totally absurd to me. The pilgrims manage to pick up forty-nine stones the night before. Not one more, not one less. Forty-nine is not a round number, and yet I learned in school that the Arabs were the first Muslims and above all, they're the ones who invented algebra. Okay, let's say the pilgrims did manage to stash away the forty-nine stones under their white robes. Why wait for the next day to go down into the plain, overheated by the sun, and then throw the forty-nine stones, one after another, at the symbols of Satan? That's called stoning. So Johnny and his terrorists are supposed to be excellent Muslims because they stoned the canine in front of all the people in the neighbourhood who, fearing reprisals, preferred to look away.

I did the same. The terrorists knew me well, as they'd slapped me a few times in the schoolyard. And their leader, Johnny the Bastard, had tripped me on the first day of school. I had the scar on my skin. My messed-up knee, that was his doing. I might've left a tooth or an eye on the field if Madame Annick or the principal hadn't ended recess. The illness that gnawed away at my bones and left me crippled probably infiltrated my body on that day. Nobody had said that. No diagnosis had been established at that time. First, because we had no access to medical care and the most elementary sanitary conditions, as you were able to have as soon as you were born in that hospital in the 12th arrondissement of Paris. Afterwards, death prowled around our heads and my parents thought that after all, polio or not, I was alive. Nobody made any connection, whether tenuous or not, between the fall, the risk of tetanus, the protective vaccine and the poliomyelitis virus. But deep down, I always knew it. Later, a few adults brought this up, often behind my back. I always knew it and I resented my parents for it. If they had administered the DTP vaccine before that fatal morning, I wouldn't be in the condition I was in.

DTP, three letters again, Béa.

D as in Diphtheria. T as in Tetanus. P as in Polio.

My life was turned upside down on that day.

First the trip-up.

Then the vaccine or rather, the absence of vaccine.

And the leg withering.

One thing followed another very fast.

All I had left were my eyes for crying.

All I could do was feed my resentment.

Ever since then, I couldn't run, or didn't know how anymore. Run again. Really run. When I'd go look for an old magazine like *Paris Match, l'Express* or an old comic book, I would take my precautions. I'd take different streets to avoid coming across hoodlums. How could I attract Amina's, Filsan's or Samia's attention? Unlike Ladane, they enjoyed reading. And how could I attract their attention without walking by the doors of their houses and raising their brothers' suspicions? I had to throw little stones against the windows of their rooms. It was a risky bet. More than once, I got beat up by some rascal who took me for a novice window-breaker. Often, as luck would have it, I fell upon an adult who punished me with a few strokes of a cane on my bottom. When I'd tell the enraged brothers that I did not lust after their sister, that I was only looking for a new adventure of Mickey Mouse or a sentimental magazine like *Nous Deux*, nobody seemed to believe me. I was harassed even more. I had to go back home dancing on one leg.

Just think, Béa, I occasionally came across that old, nameless dog—more than once. I recognized him by his filthy coat, by the big rope no longer around his neck but lying on the ground by his little spot next to Hadja Khadidja's shop. When I stared at that big, dirty rope, the whole neighbourhood seemed lifeless to me. One afternoon, I picked it up and the old dog gave me a weary look. He recognized me and did not bark. That rope symbolized our pact. It didn't matter where we came from and how we met. The dirty old dog and I formed a couple. A pitiful, crippled couple, to be sure, but a couple nonetheless. I think we accepted each other as we were. We comforted each other when we had just been assaulted by Johnny's gang. We lived in the midst of this noisy neighbourhood where nobody paid any attention to us. Worse, they kept us at a distance like lepers.

Today, I'm sure my birth brought no luck to my family. Hardly had I seen the light of day than my father came close to bankruptcy and my mother began to show signs of bewilderment. The premature death of my little sister darkened the picture. You know, Béa, that my crying threw my mother into such a state of panic that she was ready to throw me into the trash. I also learned, years later, that my father learned of my birth at the same time he learned that a big customer who owed him a lot of money had disappeared. The man had left the TFAI for an unknown destination. My father had barely escaped prison for misappropriation of funds. Was it to fill that big hole that my father worked still more and came home later and later? I pricked up my ears to hear the sound of his moped every night: it was my own, special chamber music. I would cry to stay awake and when he came in, at last, I was so out of breath I couldn't stop sobbing.

The rest was not my fault: the arguments and bitterness only concerned the adults. All Papa and Mama had to do was talk face to face and they'd say whatever they reproached the other for. Your mother and I argue, but it's never too serious, that's what they might have told me. In my childish head, it wasn't so simple. I never knew the real reasons why my parents didn't get along. There must have been deep dissatisfaction from the very start.

The old dog was far from having said his last word. And as for me, I was beginning to put words to my emotions. I was succeeding in naming things clearly, things that I was deprived of, sweet and soothing things.

The warmth of the maternal womb.

Mama's breast.

The evening porridge when I was still in her arms, before she got into the habit of passing me to another woman as if I were a cumbersome package.

The anger and impatience that rose in my chest when I could no longer stop crying.

The sputtering sounds of my father's moped when he returned home in the middle of the night.

The smell of wet earth after the first rain.

Grandma Cochise getting up at the crack of dawn, at the same time as the rooster and Ladane.

Ever since I contracted the poliovirus, I was never able to run again. And yet my head was full of dreams. At seven I could see myself as a cowboy, at twelve, I was a soccer player, at eighteen, a sailor, and at twenty-two, an author of comic books And maybe I would have become a cowboy again at thirty-five, after taking riding classes on the best stud farms. In short, my head was a mess, Béa, and I was the only one who knew it. Mama Zahra and Papa Beanpole were not the best of friends, as you know. Zahra could breathe more easily when Papa Beanpole wasn't around. Papa worked himself dizzy and came home late. And that wasn't all. The old folks didn't talk to each other often, except when they couldn't avoid it.

Like when I cried for no reason and had to shut up. For no reason? That's what they said. They weren't in my shoes. If they had been, they would have cried as much as I did, if not more. People always say, 'Put yourself in my place.' They only say it with their lips, rarely with their heart. How do I know that, Béa? Well, nobody ever offered to take my place and lend me his or hers. Nobody. There must have been a reason. They must have felt pretty good in their shoes. They probably didn't really feel like being in mine. That's what I thought and what I still think, sometimes, today. When I heard them say, 'You know what I mean, put yourself in my place', I wouldn't turn around. I went on my way. I didn't let myself get distracted by these vain words. For me, words had to keep all their meaning. What they meant had to weigh heavy on the scale, otherwise we'd all head straight for disaster. One day, Moussa Two-Oeils or someone else would yell 'Fire! Fire!' and nobody would lift a finger. And poor Moussa Two-Oeils would die right there, for want of help. Words are important. As important as water, food or the air you breathe, Béa. Our life depends on them.

Still today, words are wonderful toys. The names of certain people, certain plants, certain places or certain animals let us travel. Some words make you furious, others, joyful. You've loved the word *ceviche* ever since you tasted that Peruvian recipe. The raw fish, lemon juice and spices don't seem to aggress your adolescent palate. Of course, I didn't know ceviche at your age. Other words put my taste buds on high alert. I had the impression of leaving my little body to enter the cave of Ali Baba. Cowboy, soccer player, sailor, pilot or artist, my dreams weren't that crazy. They weren't pipe dreams either. On the contrary, they gave meaning to my life. For a while, I imagined that I'd be an infallible scientific mind that depended only on words that never lied, on well-tested calculations and graphs. 'I will be an entomologist,' I'd shout out, as a challenge to myself. The word charmed me right away. That's what we call the people who gather the names and photos of insects. In their big notebook, entomologists label each photo with the name of the insect. If they're rich, they can receive in the mail insects from the four corners of the earth. Then the entomologist can build a cabinet and place the jewel inside of it. For an entomologist, the jewel is the insect in its case. We must take care of words the way entomologists take care of their insects, pinned and glued in a big notebook called 'herbarium.'

In my neighbourhood, there was no herbarium, and the surroundings were far from tidy. Same in my family circle. My mother wanted a handsome child, vigorous and healthy, whatever its sex. Papa Beanpole wanted a great, strong boy to lead the dance of the family line. I didn't fill her desire nor his wish. I was an enigma, not the healthy older son destined for the promising future of their dreams.

For the first seven years of my life, they prayed every night to hasten the arrival of a little brother who would revenge the outrage committed on their blood. The whole neighbourhood redoubled its prayers. I had no use for their self-interested devotion. I dreamed of a little box of matches I would put away under the pile of my imaginary toys. It would nest under the red firemen's truck and my Peter Pan flute. One day it would express itself openly—that is burst into flame. It would light up the sky. As for my nice parents, they could just take to their heels. I loved that expression so much I tried to use it as much as possible and bring it up to date.

If my parents secretly prayed for another child, my aunt Dayibo prayed openly to get a rounded belly. And by imitation or contamination, I was beginning to think, often, of Nabi Issa, who is also called Christ. My great-uncle Aden's notebooks had taught me about the Nazarene. Jesus was the first to worry adults, and more generally the healthy ones. Jesus was humiliated by all the people who thought they were important because of their possessions or their offspring. He went to the very end of his quest, even if nobody wanted to follow him. From his first steps on, Jesus of Nazareth's disciples took fright. They asked him to put a definitive end to the disturbing words, the sermons and parables he kept sowing all the time. Jesus kept on with his mission. The more he preached, the more he worried those around him. His friends turned their back on him.

You disappointed us. We thought a messiah would come, not a charlatan!

He smiled at them, Béa, with his enigmatic smile. And he kept on showing the way, his way. Alone against them all. And his friends understood him, later. Once he was no longer with them. They looked for him everywhere. On dry land, on the waterways, in the caves, dark with silence. And he appeared where they expected him the least. And he renewed that experiment every time it was necessary. When I pay attention to those who surround me, I begin to understand the essence of things and of beings. The people of my neighbourhood would have behaved exactly like the Pharisees. Observing things and people, that's the key! When I managed to do it, little miracles happened. One day, as I was playing with my matchbox, fiddling with the thin wooden sticks with their dark blue tips, I realized all of a sudden that this box of matches concealed a kind of magic. Through friction, a red and yellow flame shot up and then swallowed the little wooden stick in a few seconds. The wood gave itself to the fire without hesitation and passed the relay to the wick of the lamp and the wax of the candle. The wick gave birth to light and heat. The wax burned up for all of us. Jesus, too, gave himself up completely. It took a long time for his disciples to understand him. They cursed themselves for not having tried to drink in his every word, to understand his fables and his miracles when he multiplied the loaves or the episode where he refused to send away the crowd who came to ask for him. Of course, that crowd was hungry and thirsty. Of course, five loaves and two fish were not going to satisfy such a great multitude. Yet Jesus solved the problem. The people ate and drank as they never had before. They drank and ate their fill, thanks to Jesus. They called that a miracle. More than two thousand years later, they keep calling this a miracle. But Jesus said nothing. He went on his way. He sowed hope and joy everywhere he went.

Naked joy.

Living joy.

As an adolescent, I was waiting for the little miracle that was going to come to me.

I'm still waiting for it today.

You're waiting for it too, Béa, in your own way.

It will come.

I just know it.

Something had begun to change in the way I looked at things. It was not a miracle that happened all by itself, Béa, I worked very hard at making this change. With Ladane's help, I trained myself to sharpen my attention and project myself into the future. Something changed in the way I moved, too. To me, it was obvious but I don't know if other people noticed. I felt the need to run after my mother and feverishly await the return of my father less and less. My grandmother was the only one I could rely on, as she remained exactly the same. When something was tormenting me, she welcomed me silently. And when I was lucky, she'd tell me a story. One evening when I was sick of wearing out my eyes reading an old comic book again in the half-light, she gave me a wonderful gift. And I was treated to one of the most beautiful stories in the world, Béa.

Ever since the dawn of time, men wove many legends around the three perfectly aligned stars that form the belt of Orion. They are sapphire blue. This trio is a landmark for all African nomads, and today, Grandma Cochise went on, some tribes make up pearls of stories to hang around Orion's neck. One of them is particularly charming. It's the story of a little shepherd who fell in love with those stars. He started out in life exactly like his ancestors, who were not so different from ours, except that back then the herds of giraffes, rhinoceros and elephants were so numerous they would attack their camps. What's more, our shepherd was not a good shepherd and had learned nothing from the teachings of his parents. He was not gifted at running, which is so essential to bring back the ewe or the lamb that has wandered off. He was a poor walker, too, and was easily distracted by incidents happening along the way. A wadi that flows up out of its bed, a lingering bivouac, or a quarrel around a well—it didn't take much to take him away from his work. The other shepherds made no bones about calling him a sissy. One day, he met a man who was coming back from the city. There was something about him that set him apart from all the other troubadours he'd met on the stony trails. This man had a little metallic box protected by a black plastic case in the left-hand pocket of his long shirt. It kept him company and he seemed to hold it dear, like his best ewe or some creature resembling us. For days and weeks, the young shepherd kept turning around the troubadour like a starving hyena circling its victim. Touched by his perseverance, the stranger finally told him that the precious box contained what he called 'the telescope' and sometimes he connected to the heavens simply through the magic of this optical instrument or, more precisely, of its polished lenses.

He added knowingly that the world he was discovering thanks to the telescope was his, and he was the only one to know and visit it, without having to ask for permission. The little shepherd became the friend of the man with the telescope. And from chatting with him about this and that, he also became a friend of the optical instrument. Sometimes he, too, put it on his right eye. Then on his left eye. The telescope was light and that surprised him greatly. So it didn't have much in its belly. But far from reducing its attraction, its lightness made it more desirable. It was easy to maintain: an infant could take care of it correctly. At night, under the heavens with a thousand stars, nothing is more exalting, more exotic than that universe which seemed to contain all the others: lands, continents, and oceans. After this discovery, he completely lost interest in chasing the sheep and goats, to the great despair of his family, especially his mother. Determined to earn his living quickly, in order to reassure his nomad parents, the little shepherd made his way to the city. He had ruminated on his decision like an old camel who has nothing to fear from people anymore. He was aware, however, that the task would not be easy for him, especially at the start. But he was sufficiently confident in his lucky star. And the telescope confirmed his trust. One night, it whispered to him that he should leave for the city and that he would likely do great things there.

Now there he was, in Djibouti.

Grandma Cochise skips over the journey, the stopover for a few weeks at Ali-Sabieh and the torments of thousands of young people from the brush washed up in town before him.

Like them, he learned to stretch out his piece of cardboard to sleep on at night in front of the warehouses of the port. During the day, they carried bags of merchandise on their backs. They washed or relieved themselves in the sea. They were so close to the maritime element that they ended up forgetting their former lives, the flock and the transhumance. Some only ate the flesh of fish that their parents would have vomited up immediately. Grandma Cochise assured me that the shepherd who loved the stars became a great sailor and made a fortune in pearls. Others were less lucky. In Ethiopia, it was not rare to kidnap little shepherds and castrate them to serve as eunuchs at the monarch's court. If our little shepherd had escaped this miserable fate, it's because he could raise his head to heaven and dream big.

Grandma Cochise always told me stories to entertain me but also to instil in me the right reflexes to adopt in life. She hit the bull's eye! The stories had the effect of breaking through my shell. I would have so loved Mama to do the same but that was too much to ask. If my mother lacked the emotional resources to do her job of being a mum right, it is perhaps because she never had her own mother's attention. I imagine my mother found herself alone in her room in the maternity ward with her first child—me—in her bony arms. I suppose she then realized that she had the full responsibility for a human being! As she had not received the maternal love of her own mother very early on, my mother had not learned to nourish such a skinny little baby. Would she have breasts large enough to satisfy the hungry being that had just left her belly? I suppose my mother finally saw she had a human being beside her. She was gripped with panic. She stuck her head in the sand. Is maternal instinct acquired or is it innate, as some adults seem to think to reassure themselves? I had no idea. I was just a mouth to be fed, a tiny being seeking caresses and kisses. We gave you this primordial love. In every region of the world, a baby who is normally desired and conceived has a right to warm baths and massages given by the mother. This care and attention is sometimes taken over by aunts after a difficult childbirth, or one that is dangerous for her or the child. One thing is certain: Grandma Cochise inherited from her mother a good maternal instinct. She must have known the tree under which her placenta was buried half an hour after her birth. She had to water it for seven years as tradition demanded. Not my mother. And that changes everything, don't you think, Béa?

In the fall of 1981, four years after Djibouti had gained its independence, my mother had given birth to a little sister, Fathia, who gave her back her smile. Ossobleh was growing up and I had just entered a brand-new middle school. I had matured in the course of those three months of vacation. True, the cyclone had ravaged my neighbourhood, but it had made us stronger and more supportive of each other. Every time I tried to follow her, Ladane would quicken her pace, leaving behind her only a cloud of dust. Her little game no longer amused me. I learned to guess, Béa, what was hidden behind my grandmother's silence. I learned to unravel the threads of time suspended between the banks of the present and of the past. To see the difference between what I was observing around me and what I was discovering in a book. Driven by my curiosity and fired up by Cochise's stories, I succeeded in crossing the fragile bridge that went from the real world to the world we call invisible.

To please my French teacher in eighth grade, Madame Ellul, I read voraciously during and after class. I arrived in class with many well-sharpened pencils as ammunition. Madame Ellul understood my state of mind very well. She appreciated my compositions, inspired either by imaginary characters like the hunchback Quasimodo, or historical figures like Cleopatra, whose nose changed the face of the world. As the weeks went by, my pen grew livelier. It could now tackle social topics, leave the familiar coastline to go land on the banks of the world. I began to blacken pages on the question of paid vacations, on the Gestapo, on snow in the Pyrenees or on Cannes and the Côte d'Azur. Most of my fellow students thought my choice of subjects exotic. They wrote slapdash compositions. Not me. I applied myself, so as to put into practice the advice the teacher had given us and everyone else seemed to have forgotten. My teacher's advice is still extremely useful to me. It will be useful to you, too, someday, Béa, I'm sure of it. Okay, for you I will disclose just three of the pieces of advice she gave us:

Respect punctuation and the rules of grammar.

Alternate short sentences and long ones to create rhythm.

Use your knowledge and, if you get stuck, your imagination.

At the beginning of the school year, Madame Ellul had us copy out her rules, underline them in green and circle those three precious sentences. The first time I succeeded in slipping a paragraph from Daudet's *Monsieur Seguin's Last Kid Goat* into my composition, Madame Ellul invited me to the sixth-grade class so I could dialogue with her students. I was so proud of my prowess before these kids, some of whom had been mean to me outside. I could still hear the flattering words of the teacher. In my composition, M. Seguin's goat was a goat grazing on the cardboard boxes and plastic wires of our neighbourhood, but it remained as playful and naughty as its distant ancestor. Madame Ellul was moved, and quoted, with sparkling eyes, the whole paragraph inspired by M. Alphonse Daudet, whose works I had unearthed at the *Centre Culturel Français Arthur-Rimbaud* (CCFAR):

'...Oh! how pretty she was, M. Seguin's little goat.'

How pretty she was, with her gazelle's eyes, her soft goatee, her black, gleaming hoofs, her pointed horns and her long, hairy coat that gave her a diabolical look!

And then, docile, cheerful and charming, letting herself be milked without budging and without putting her hoof in the pail...

The title of my composition was *A Darling Little Goat*. She loved it and she found my conclusion, in the form of a punch line, quite relevant.

My reputation spread beyond the walls of the Boulaos Middle School. As my school compositions took up a large part of my time, I no longer wrote the administrative letters I used to write to make my parents' life easier. Our neighbours had soon realized that I was a kind of public letter-writer. One day I had to compose a letter of complaint for an aunt, the next day an impassioned missive for a pal who wanted to attract the favours of the sister of one of my schoolmates who'd gone on from the Château-d'Eau school to Boulaos Middle School like me.

Goodbye letters, hello imagination.

Madame Ellul's attention gave me a great push. When she read aloud with emotion in her voice and a spot of fire sparkling in her hazel eyes, it propelled me into another universe. From one day to the next, I became a celebrity in the whole school.

Lots of boys sought out my company now and some girls looked at me in a way that touched me. In the neighbourhood, too, my reputation was preceded by a flattering rumour. Boosted by the legend, it rose like the dough Hashim the baker kneaded with his skinny fingers. They said I knew how to make all the famous people of history come to life. And that Emperor Haile Selassie and the Queen of Sheba owed part of their glory to me. And I knew how to embalm the recumbent statues of the Ambouli cemetery in the sweet, silky French language.

My success had its drawbacks. Some tough guys, the school bigshots, decided to use my services. They'd send me the subject of the composition that had given them nightmares, one or two days before it was due. I had to get that thorn out of their side. In exchange, they'd make sure I was safe this school year and the next. Their solicitude flattered me, even if sometimes I had to rack my brains to fill their sheet of paper. They didn't care much about the content. Happy as long as their two pages of double-spaced paper were covered with my twisty handwriting. I suspected, Béa, that those bullies were mostly appreciative of my long words. As soon as I realized they loved long, pompous terms, I drew up a list of adverbs, each stretched out longer than the next. Slipping in an *obstinately* or an *unfortunately* right from the introduction filled me with joy and confirmed my statute as Champion of Letters.

From churning out so many pages for those hoods, my mind sometimes went into a slump. Sank into quicksand without finding a cure for my writer's block. Went around in circles for a few days. You know what, Béa? Once again, the solution came all by itself. A detail attracted my attention while I was skimming through a book I had never opened before. A thin book that managed to escape my thirst for reading, or a fat one with a binding that had been quietly sleeping on a bookshelf of the CCFAR. The detail would pop up most often in the middle of a new story. At other times, a comic-book hero I liked most particularly (hey! a long adverb) came to the rescue. It spared me embarrassment and the wrath of the bully, who cared about his reputation, too. Before Asterix, Lucky Luke, Tintin and Achille Talon, I was familiar with other memorable heroes. Tough guys like Blek the Rock, Rahan or Tarzan. Sometimes an episode stolen from some comic book or other inspired me to flesh out my prose for one of the big shots. My method was refined over time. I would weave a tale, follow its thread wherever my imagination led me, and then pore over the last part with particular care. My conclusion? A little moral tale inspired by the topic of the composition, and bingo!

Like a chef, I cooked up the same invented story in various sauces. I served the same rearranged dish to various bullies. In my last two years of middle school, I regularly slipped dozens of compositions to various big shots, not counting the poor guys who dropped by late at my house in hopes of softening me up. They cried and swore on the head of their mother they had a comp due early the next day and they'd sweated over it for days and nights without finding the slightest idea or putting the first sentence down on paper. These poor guys kept saying that I was the lucky one because ideas came to me easily and sentences flowed effortlessly from my fingers. All I had to do was give them five little minutes and by the grace of God the paper would fill up all by itself. I sent them packing. If they kept bugging me, I could always give their names to one of the big bullies.

One day, I provoked a scandalous incident, according to the words of the teacher who read and annotated a composition whose author I was. I had written it for a fearsome bully with tense lips. The guy was known for his fits of temper and his OCD. Three letters easy to remember: Obsessive Compulsive Disorder.

The topic of the composition was on the dangers of the prostitution that was affecting our city—more particularly, some former students attracted by the high life and easy money. Instead of taking on a hard, reproving tone, the bully's paper was rather complacent. From there to suspecting the bully of celebrating vice, there was only a step and the teacher almost took it. He read the passage that incriminated the suspect with a disgusted air:

'Oh the girls of my country are so pretty
Lye-lye-lye-lye-lye
Yes they're so pretty, the girls of my country
Lye-lye-lye-lye-lye
The sun of the summer nights
Shines in their eyes.'

When the incident reached the principal's ears, there were two or three teachers who pleaded irony, something the bully hardly appreciated. Perhaps Madame Ellul recognized my style, for she pleaded my cause and refreshed the memory of the obtuse teacher. She explained that the song by Enrico Macias was about French Algeria. The bully was exonerated on the spot. He came to my house to inform me of the verdict. A crowd of kids accompanied him. I savoured my victory with restraint. Actually, Béa, I exulted, but without showing it. The big shot shook my hand for what seemed an eternity. He explained that he'd been very angry because they had dragged him in the mud but he was also very proud of having been exonerated by a jury made up of French-from-France. He said again not to worry about my protection. I was safe, my reputation was settled, I had nothing to prove anymore. After this incident, I scrawled out fewer compositions. I devoted myself to my own inventions. At the end of the school year, I got my middle school diploma with honours and also passed the entry into the tenth grade. Four of the big shots got their middle school diplomas, too, but were not admitted into high school. Without a diploma, the fifth one joined the army, which was recruiting a lot of young people to make up for the departure of the French volunteer personnel of the TFAI. At the time, there was just one lycée, Béa. Getting into it changed your life. Once there, you felt you'd gained access to a very selective club. After the lycée, you were part of the country's elite. You could choose to remain and serve in the administration, or leave for France to go to university.

While waiting to enter high school, I kept reading and writing little comic poems. Just to amuse or console myself. I occupied a corner of the only table in the house. Completely taken up by the infant, my mother no longer put a damper on my penchant for reading and writing. She no longer worried about my eyes. Ladane continued to raise little clouds of dust in her wake. For the first time in my life, I felt cramped in the narrow little streets of my neighbourhood, that confined space where my preoccupations kept going around in circles. I spent my weekends at the CCFAR, three kilometres from my dead-end street. And for once, I ate up the distance. If I had a crazy leg, as they said, I did not have broken wings. And still less a rusty brain. I had started an epistolary relationship with characters from the past. If I were in the same situation today, I would have written to Barack Obama and Pope Francis. I also would have written a lovely letter to your mama Margherita, who must have been just starting out in primary school in Milan, her native city.

Here I am, among the elite. In high school. I'm a *lycéen* now. After two or three years, I could have taken the competitive exam that gets you into the administration of the Post Office, or into Customs, even without a high school diploma. I could have helped my family. Papa Beanpole thought I could be a schoolteacher. The salary was pretty good, and then there were the three months of vacation when I could have traded the intense heat of Djibouti for the open, healthy air of Addis Ababa, the capital of neighbouring Ethiopia. He'd cited the case of a cousin who had gone from schoolteacher to principal in a few years and then built a real house for his old parents. I had made a note of it that day but then switched very quickly to another subject of conversation. My father didn't insist; it wasn't like him to repeat things. He kept his thoughts to himself. I suspected him of brooding in silence. To tell the truth, he had other things to worry about. He was getting old. He attracted illnesses like a magnet attracts iron filings. Diabetes, hypertension and headaches, not to mention the damage tuberculosis had done to his bronchial tubes. He did not complain, however, never dwelt on his own health but worried about his mother, who was confined to bed. Every week, he went half-heartedly to the great Friday prayer, more out of duty than anything else.

Papa Beanpole gave the impression of moving among shadows, of ignoring the hassles of daily life. My mother Zahra, on the other hand, ran on torments and permanent worry while nursing a third little sister named Safia. When the old man came down on earth again, he would poke fun at her, the better to push away his own fears. Discreet—secretive, in fact—he wasn't the kind to pour out his emotions. He remained dignified before his children. Many years later, as I hadn't managed to straddle his old moped, which Ossobleh drove with one hand, he gave me this little life lesson:

'Don't worry, we end up acquiring reflexes, even for riding a bike.'

I didn't have reflexes, but I gained confidence instead. Hardly had I arrived at the Djibouti lycée than I found solid allies among the teachers. My first essay impressed the faculty, as I learned later. Madame Lequellec, my French teacher in tenth grade, who knew Madame Ellul well, invited me to join the lycée's reading club. It was a literary circle frequented by many female students, a number of them from France and other European countries, and it impressed me from the very first day. We spent Monday and Wednesday afternoons in groups of two or three, reading and rereading the fantastic tales of Maupassant and Edgar Allan Poe, reciting aloud poems by Baudelaire, the dandy poet, venturing into the labyrinths of the *Arabian Nights,* and writing notes on our readings. Subsequently, I realised I could talk with these sophisticated readers without stammering. Two weeks later, I met the team of the lycée's newspaper. As a sign of welcome, they published my first article, an imaginary letter to Anne Frank.

'Dear Anne Frank,

You were plunged into darkness. I know you were hungry and thirsty. All around you, silence, silence, silence. In the distance, a faint noise is perceptible from time to time. The wind, timidly blowing. You were waiting for the claw of fear to fade away or disappear as hunger progressively took over.

I got your last message. It reached me easily. I will waste no time answering you. When the flesh is pushed to the wall, it finally bites back. There are days when someone who never talks ends up talking under torture.

Dear Anne, you're probably no longer in this world but I'm going to keep writing to you because your absence is not a sufficient reason to stop conversing with you.

And it would be indelicate of me.

I refuse to give in to that feeling, which has no place in my language. What's more, you are still present in my heart, and how could I forget that.

I was told, Anne, that a small museum has just acquired your most accomplished work. It bears your lip prints. Which has the effect of shutting up the expert auctioneers who doubted your talent and even your existence; those jerks have no shame! I speak from experience. There were thousands of buyers in the auction room, said the Amsterdam press. Mainly a crowd of rich, beautiful women, wearing custom-made designer clothes. It was a red-letter day for them. They had rented the services of paparazzi, but they pretended to ignore them in public. You can bet most of those women set foot in that room for the first time.

Your loving friend.'

I always had a ready answer for Monsieur Blanchard, my philosophy teacher. That subject set my whole body on fire. Life and death, freedom and responsibility, happiness or its absence—no subject ever seemed too abstract or scholastic. It was all fascinating to me. I think, Béa, that I charmed Monsieur Blanchard and my classmates in the last year of high school with my curiosity and conceptual agility. The stoics, the hedonists and the cynics kept me company. Socrates above all, my new hero. In my neighbourhood, bringing up Plato's master was a source of misunderstanding. My former middle school classmates would go off about the exploits of Socrates, the captain of the Brazilian football team. Many aficionados (and I was one of them) knew the interminable name of that midfielder by heart: Socrates Brasileiro Sampaio de Souza Vieira de Oliveira. You can see why everybody just used his first name.

I shouldn't make fun of my former friends. They had changed. Or rather, I was the one who had changed a great deal. You couldn't see it at first glance. Understandably—everything that's too small for the naked eye, like microbes, we try to magnify it with tools like a microscope. Everything that's too far away, like clouds or stars, we shrink it onto a sheet of graph paper. We call that knowledge. We spend years sitting at a desk in school to acquire it. In my adolescence, some were able to get it without going through school. Others assimilated it in the street because they had to survive. Because they had their family to feed. All the boys of my age were dismissed from school very young. All of them had now a family to support. I knew some who'd gone to work at the slaughterhouse. I would meet them carrying meat carcasses for butchers who paid them in kind. The offal sold very well in our neighbourhoods. These boys, whom I called survivors, had a well-oiled technique: they'd put the heads and hooves of sheep and goats on one side and the heads and hooves of cows on the other. They'd wrap up the two lots and before ten they were back in the hood. The housewives who'd placed their order the day before sent out their maids to get the still quivering meat. On the mornings I didn't go to school, I enjoyed watching the maids carving out and boning the meat. Ripping out the nerves on the first try even with a very sharp knife was no easy job. Not easy either to rip out chunks of meat from the bones.

I didn't see Ladane very much anymore. In addition to her domestic chores, she was taking care of my grandmother who was now disabled. I spent most of my time at school or at the CCFAR.

I had no intention of making fun of my former classmates when they confused the ancient philosopher with the football player born in Belem. That was their problem, not mine. They had made fun of the way I walked before. I chose to be quiet about their ignorance and spare them my mockery.

I often took the bus to school. Sometimes, I walked there or came back on foot without interrupting my inner conversation with Cicero or Marcus Aurelius. Their advice never seemed too different from the advice of my grandmother, who taught me to fight. Yes, it was really Cochise who first taught me not to consider myself a cripple.

Handicapped.

A victim.

I contracted polio as a child.

I am no longer that kid.

I never again let myself be defined by this illness or by any other.

Why should poliomyelitis define me and not hay fever, the flu or mumps? From my grandmother's teachings, I took away the lesson that in life, all is only movement. I realized that Heraclitus of Ephesus said exactly that. The points of convergence were not lacking. And there were more surprises in store for me. With a philosophy book in my hand, I'd go through two or three neighbourhoods, slowly, with short steps, until I stumbled upon the gates of the lycée. In the evening, I would go back the other way. Why take the bus, Béa? Socrates, Rousseau and Kant loved to walk. They philosophised as they walked. I imitated them and saved a few pennies. Once I got home, I'd find Cochise wasting away under my very eyes. It made me sick.

A few days later, my grandmother died. I had feared her death like no other in the world. No, you can't say I was surprised. The earth gave way under my feet, Béa. Socrates' suicide had left its mark on me, but it hadn't touched the bottom of my heart. And I never had Socrates' features printed on my retina. I imagined him as he could appear to me according to the legend. A bull-necked man of medium height, wearing a white tunic, who had the habit of stopping idlers in the middle of Athens. But ancient Greece was not exactly next door. The pain I felt when my beloved Cochise died was another story.

Grandma died in her sleep.

Grandma Cochise is no more.

For me, nothing will ever be the way it was before.

She was born about twenty years after the inauguration of the famous canal in 1869. The man who had imagined digging up the earth at this strategic spot to connect the Red Sea and the Mediterranean was a French engineer, Ferdinand de Lesseps. I knew his name because it was the name the French had given to the first middle school in the TFAI.

According to my grandmother, who had her own calendar, the renovation of the port of Djibouti dated back to the birth of her last child, who was born dead but could have become my paternal uncle if God had given him life. My grandmother stressed that although no one spoke about it back then, the Suez Canal was not progress, as the Paris newspapers claimed. What kind of progress was that? Hundreds of thousands of Egyptian peasants transformed into masons and road workers were carried off. What was this progress that had ripped tons of sand from the sea? What was this progress that had brought with it new illnesses like dysentery and cholera? Not one of our ancestors was happy with it. Not one. Worse, hardly had the first boat floated on the brand-new canal that the English and the French spoiled the festivities with their rivalry. The British troops drove out the Ottomans and occupied Egypt. Then, before the end of the First World War, in which first cousins of my grandmother Cochise fought, the English and the French signed the Sykes-Picot agreement that allowed them to share the whole region. Grandma told me it was Monsieur Picot who signed it for France and Mister Sykes represented the Queen of England. Of course, the agreement was secret and no one was to talk about it, at least back then. Especially not our ancestors, the nomads who wandered across a vast region along the Red Sea to the other side facing the Indian Ocean, where our cousins in Somalia lived. Grandma Cochise never opened a book in her life, for she did not know how to read and write, but she had the memory of an elephant, like the storytellers of ancient times. Everything she'd heard during her long life was saved on her hard drive and so the day she would leave us, by an act of the Lord or Satan, would be a great tragedy. It would be as if the whole library of my childhood neighbourhood went up in smoke. When Cochise heard an anecdote, you may be sure, Béa, that she saved it carefully in her brain.

She was just a wisp of a woman now, almost a phantom.

A little heap of bones, no more than sixty or seventy pounds.

She went unnoticed, except for her large imploring eyes.

Her cavernous voice and her face, motionless, expressionless, but serene.

Certainly not the look of a mad pigeon: people destroyed by the inner struggle playing out in the hollow of their guts and looking for a way out sometimes have that look.

A struggle long hidden from her family, more persistent than an old tune...

She's no longer here and all is sad and grey.

As promised, I've told you, in my turn and by fragments, the stories my beloved Grandmother used to tell me. The history of the *Côte Française des Somalis* as well as the story of the *Territoire Français des Afars et des Issas*. CFS. TFAI. Those abbreviations were part of my childhood even if I was too young to connect myself directly to the CFS, which became the TFAI two years after I was born. At her side, my mind was frolicking over the great meadows surrounding the famous canal. The dreams of my childhood were populated by governors, missionaries and French explorers like Ferdinand de Lesseps and Charles de Foucault. The landscape of my childhood is dotted with Lorraine Crosses and Legionnaires' kepis. In the background, there is the voice of General de Gaulle as well as the voices of his lieutenants, who you never heard of. Their names were Messmer, Malraux, Debré, Peyrefitte... For a long time, I stayed in Cochise's wake. As a teenager, I would fall asleep to the sound of her gently hissing voice. I loved her musky smell when she bent down to blow out the candle. My little heart raced when she promised to tell me the story of the journey of her cousins who enlisted to fight alongside the French troops in the Great War. My status of a sick, feverish child gave me certain privilege, which I had no intention of passing up.

Grandma Cochise was no longer in this world when three weeks later, I got my Baccalauréat in Philosophy. I missed getting it with Highest Honors by five points. I couldn't have cared less. To overcome my grief, I recalled the nights spent under Cochise's skirt. Every night of my childhood and adolescence, there was the same intoxication, the same delight. The same galloping backwards into the times gone by. Carried away by the urge to tell her stories, Grandma would forget the time slipping through our fingers. Hardly had she caught her breath that we were at the gates of dawn. She'd collapse on her rush mat and snore like your grandfather Amine's moped.

Grandma Cochise was no longer there to take me in her arms. She was no longer there to praise me in her rough way. I left for France to continue my studies. I packed up and left as soon as the summer of 1985 ended. I left my mother and four brothers and sisters behind me. I left Papa Beanpole shaken by cough, with tears in his eyes. The cavernous echo of his fits of coughing haunted me for a long time. And I left, abandoning all the memories of my neighbourhood. I was selfish. I wanted to save my skin. I left everything behind me, Béa. To one and all, I said: 'Ciao, ciao, ciao!'

I never slept so well in my life as in the week I arrived in France. This sleep was precious but it had a price, too. The first days, I did not get out of bed unscathed. It was as if parts of me remained glued in sleep. As if my brain was stagnating, macerating in the fog, ignorant of the place it was in. We were in September and the lengthening of the days was disturbing my inner compass, stuck as it was on the Djibouti sun, whose daily course ends before 6pm. For five whole days, I swam in cottony indolence, and when I managed to extricate myself, it was only to sink back into it immediately. My limbs moved slowly; words would not come to me, nor would sensations. I willingly skipped meals. I missed the open hours of the student cafeteria more than once. All I could do was grab some yoghurts and bananas at the nearest grocery.

My student's room at Mont-Saint-Aignan was clean, modest, and just like all the others. It looked onto a garden surrounded by football fields and tennis courts. The temperate climate of Normandy, humid and oceanic, upset my biological clock. A few days or a few weeks later, I managed to get used to it. I threw myself into the frenetic life of a student, going from the lecture hall to the student cafeteria, from the dorms to the athletic field. In Djibouti, the students at the lycée knew, vicariously, the rites and rhythms of this bubbling life. For weeks before my departure for Rouen, I had studied every detail of it. I was not disappointed. The rustic harmony of Mont-Saint-Aignan struck me from the start. Once the picturesque charm of the old town had somewhat faded, the rest of the landscape gave me the impression of a green savannah, streaked with rails and high-tension wires, where one-time lovers could hide at night.

I had a room of my own for the first time in my life. Cloistered in this room, I took refuge in dreaming and its corollary, reading. And, just for fun at first, I began to set my thoughts down on paper. I would usually write at night, when the dorm was silent. Writing was an obligation, a quasi-biological way of breathing, of experiencing by proxy what I imagined was happening in Rouen as well as out there in Djibouti. I went from one period of my life to the other, from one bank of the sea to the other, without any apparent effort, sliding along the meanders of my imagination until the early hours of the morning, numb with sleep.

Besides the bed and the little sink, my simple room had a desk, for me and just for me. Under that desk, there were two drawers. The right-hand drawer received my reports and essays to be returned to the professors. The left-hand one, my personal drafts. During the day, I kept my right hemisphere active. At night, I would sink into the wrinkles and folds of my left hemisphere. When an idea had been trotting through my head for weeks, I knew it deserved a little niche in my unploughed nocturnal fields. Now, Béa, I know that when I set out to cover sheets of paper with black scribble, I was looking for the land where my dream house would stand. I was constructing narratives that would enrich myself with everything we can't do without. Everything I had already lost. I had left a country and the people I loved. I had, above all, broken up with my childhood. At night, I was unaware that my tears would flow at the mere thought of the soft rustling of my Château-d'Eau neighbourhood.

I was studying for the final exams that counted for the DEUG, the exam that would get me into my second year, when I learned the terrible news. Ladane had committed suicide. In my country, women overwrought by misery take their life in the worst way possible: by fire. Ladane had done it. No one had been able to save her. I'd had no news of her since I left more than two years earlier. I knew nothing of her fate, Béa. Had she been raped in a dark alley by a horde of drunken legionnaires? Did her parents throw her into the arms of an old man with several families already? Was she betrayed by a small-time prince charming?

Never did I learn what kind of misfortune Ladane the maid had to face. No one will raise the wedding flag for her. That custom, which has been abandoned in the villages and remote oases of my country, was the secret dream of every young woman ever since matchmakers had become rare. A red flag was chosen when the fiancée was under twenty, blue up to thirty and yellow beyond. The time of the red flag was the time of carefreeness. The blue banner was a synonym for impatience mixed with worry. With the yellow flag, they were hanging onto the rails of hope. There was always something exceptional in that last zone of waiting. On nights when the moon was full, pacts were made with djinns. In mystical conclaves, women would sing out heart-rending airs, supported by the beating and jangling of the tambourine. The preparations of amulets, the magic of oil lamps, the goatskin talismans buried in the houses and destined to 'open' the womb of women who had remained sterile... Ladane would never know that whole hodgepodge of superstitions. She would not test the formulas capable of renewing a husband's ardour, of bringing him back to his bed at the side of his wife, excised since adolescence. She would not recite the prayers meant to round out her belly or precipitate her offspring into the invisible world of the ancestors sleeping in the sanctuary just outside the village. She would not dry out like my aunt Dayibo, who multiplied her consultations with the fortune-teller to hear her invariably predict a happy event. Your home will resound with the joyful cries of a pudgy baby, the soothsayer predicted.

   I never knew what had driven Ladane to take her life, Béa. She was twenty-one. If I were a sculptor, I would have modelled Ladane's silhouette. She would have a bucket in her right hand, a child on her back, and firewood on her head. She would be seven months pregnant. She would have a bunch of kids who would give her other kids. She would be a hundred years old.

They called me Jack Lang.

The Djiboutian students, both the ones I spent time with in Rouen and the ones I met in Paris, had lost nothing of their cutting humour. Very quickly, they found a nickname for me that was both flattering and caustic. On the one hand, they acknowledged my literary and artistic inclination. Hadn't François Mitterrand's flamboyant Minister of Culture, Jack Lang, become, in everyone's eyes, in France and abroad, the best ambassador of French language and culture? On the other hand, through a cleverly balanced translinguistic play on words, they emphasised my difference: *Langaareh* in Somali, my mother tongue, means someone who's lame. Now I was an artist—and lame.

The nickname followed me when I left the university. Married, the father of two boys, I was a teacher by day and a writer at night. My old friends saw me every now and then. They heard me talk about my books on the radio or on TV. It was now perfectly obvious: I had become a strange animal. A silhouette, a name. Books. Travel. No doubt about it, they thought, I wasn't quite like them anymore. I had become someone else. I deserved my nickname and they were happy for me.

So Jack Lang it is.
And sometimes just Jack.
I had no choice.
I accepted that new coat
philosophically.
Proudly, too.
I had become a chameleon,
From here and from elsewhere.
Walking and dancing,

Dancing and amusing the crowd,
a strange animal,
An inspired, unpredictable Janus,
Increasingly restless.
African one day, French the next.
A Norman, to boot.
So I'm Jack Lang.
Jack the flamboyant, Langaareh the lame.
But there's something better—writing: my homeland.
My books: my passport.
The labour of days, the labour of nights.
The pen tore up the masks that veiled my silhouette.
Casting off, setting sail.
Nothing would ever stop me.

I met your mother Margherita six years before you were born. It was in Rome, the city of eternal love. I had just turned forty. I was a dashing forty-year-old and I had already written several novels. Your mother, Béa, was so beautiful she looked as if she'd just stepped out of a painting by Raphael, but don't worry, she's as splendid now as she was on that very first day. I was starting the promotional tour for the translation of my fourth novel into the language of Dante. I was to meet the press and give a public reading as part of a series of gatherings called 'Reading Africa', before going to Bologna and Torino.

I met Margherita in a very small bookstore devoted to the arts and literature of the African continent that your mother had the good idea of starting, with the help of a few women friends of hers. You're going to tell me you know all that already, Béa. But your mamma couldn't—or wouldn't—tell you that behind the artistic pretext for the Libreria Ebano, there was another, more prosaic reason: give an occupation to Carlotta, your future grandmother, newly retired and so prone to melancholy. Carlotta cursed Roman life, too exhausting for her taste. She wasn't wrong, you know. Arguing with a taxi driver is enough to ruin the reputation of the papal city. A thousand jokes about the Romans are always going around in Italy. They make fun of those crude, impatient, loudmouths. Everything about the Romans is a source of laughter—their dirtiness, for starters. My favourite joke sounds like a riddle. I'll give it to you verbatim:

Who's more useless than a garbage collector in Rome? Einstein in the land of charlatans. From that, the jokes are strung together like pearls in a necklace. Who's more religious than a Roman? Another Roman, of course!

Carlotta ended up leaving Rome for Milan, where Margherita was born. We go there as often as possible. From the time you were very young, we travelled a lot so your tastes and your curiosity could resonate with the diversity and the mysteries of the world. We wanted you to grow up with a wanderer's spirit. Do you remember David and Abigail, the researchers from Boston? The couple who lived with us when you were five or six? You were very attached to them. From the very first day, you turned on the charm and in a very short time became their accomplice. Hardly had they set down their bags that you bombarded them with questions about their clothes, their country, and what they usually ate. Some people, Béa, are deeply moved by the reality of others, by their way of speaking or lighting a cigarette, or by their table manners. There are others who observe the world with a detached eye. You obviously belong to the first circle. You welcomed our American friends. You were playful and teasing, like when one of your friends came to sleep over. Sometimes they didn't answer you because they didn't know what to say. Once, when you asked them if they'd seen me biking in the streets of Boston, where I'd lived for two semesters just after meeting your mother, their silence grew heavier. You pretended not to notice their embarrassment. Then you tried again, *diretto*, as if nothing was the matter.

Americans are very gentle, especially with children. They'd listened attentively to your questions all week, prompting you with the English words missing from the vocabulary of a naughty little girl. We, your mother and I, did notice their confusion. From her post at the stove, while peeling succulent Sicilian tomatoes, Margherita was eavesdropping. As for me, I didn't want to butt in. I limited myself to my role as host first, then guide. I wanted them to see the new Parisian spot, from Saint-Ouen to the fallow fields of Bercy. I must confess you had caught me off guard. I hadn't imagined for a second that you were going to ask about my competence as a cyclist. You wanted to know if they'd seen me pedalling in the Boston suburbs. I can tell you the answer Abigail and Dave couldn't have given you. The answer is no. At five, you couldn't be clear about it so your curiosity was natural. What's more, you had never seen me on a bike or a scooter. Nor on a ski slope. Now you know the answer. No, I still don't know how to ride a bike and I never had the courage to venture out on a skateboard. The polio that weakened my right leg at the age of seven kept me from all those activities. But, as a bonus, I inherited that rolling gait. I don't know how to ride a bike. But I like to dance. As a student in Rouen, I sometimes danced in front of the windowpane in the hall of my dorm, with a comb stuck in my Afro. Oblivious of everything else, I swayed my hips to the rhythm of the dense moaning of Otis Redding or the meowing of Michael Jackson.,

Yes I like to dance.
So I dance.
I dance even when I walk.
Without thinking about it.
It's second nature.
It's my signature.

For three nights in a row, Abigail, Dave and I went club hopping. The last night, just before their departure at dawn for Logan airport, we had the time of our lives. On a barge transformed into a nightclub, we had the privilege of admiring liana-women parading before us. Each more beautiful than the last. Perched on geisha shoes that made them look like ibises on springs. I'm telling you about the ibis, Béa, because you've loved that royal bird ever since you discovered it at the Paris zoo when you were little. After the barge closed, we took a taxi for a last turn around the dance floor. There, we danced, again and again, jumping in the air like little brats leaving the schoolyard on the last day of the school year. No point apologizing when you bumped into someone in the crowd: the electro music was so loud that it covered the sounds and isolated the concert hall from the neighbourhood around the Bastille. Stromae didn't have to ask us to dance. As soon as we recognized the first measures of his hit *Alors on danse* we threw ourselves onto the dance floor and never left it.

No need for encouragement.

I dance as I walk.

I walk as I dance.

It's lasted for over 38 years.

I've fully accepted my rolling walk.

To say it in Stromae's words, I find myself fantastic.

Fantastic, and absolutely not pathetic.

In the midst of the crowd, I had eyes only for Stromae's choreography. I knew every step, every move of the hips, every mimic of the half Rwandan-half Flemish maestro. Let me make one last confession, Béa. I had met Stromae in Rio two or three years before. We even had kept a little epistolary relationship everyone thought flattering for me. Stromae was friendly enough to send me an invitation card from Brussels. This whimsical artist is a man of his word. He had promised he'd invite me as soon as he was back in Paris. And he kept his word.

The winks of the gazelles had no effect on my friends and me. We were there to sweat blood and dance till the small hours of the morning. I don't know if Stromae saw us. We danced like crazy, my little group and I. Our fervour increased tenfold when Stromae asked the crowd what piece they wanted to hear. Like one man, the crowd shouted: 'Papaoutai.' This piece works like a charm. It opens hearts and unites parents and kids. Of course, the audience took up the song a cappella. Everyone knew the words. I know you love that song, too, Béa. When I was away, you'd sing it to me on Skype. Whether or not Stromae spurred us to dance, I thought of you on the dance floor, my darling. I had you under my skin, my sweet little girl!

Where's your dad?
Tell me where's your dad?
Without even having to talk to him
He knows what's wrong
Oh my dear father

I was mad with joy, yelling along with the overheated audience. David and Abigail were in heaven, too. We applauded so much our hands were numb for a long time after the piece ended.

Suddenly, I thought of my parents. My mother's features came into focus on my retina, like a non-digital photo fresh out of the stop bath. I think she was encouraging me to keep on clapping. My father looked hieratic, silently staring at me with his watery, old man's eyes. Our non-verbal exchange stretched out and deepened. At his sides, my Grandma Cochise and my aunt were conferring. They were blessing me, I think. In the background, Ladane was there, too. Luminous. She winked at me and then sent me a burst of positive vibes, to use one of your favourite expressions. Too bad you and Margherita couldn't witness my emotion at that moment. You were fast asleep. Margherita in foetal position and you, surrounded by your two cuddly elephants with Obama-like ears.

I danced a saraband with my parents.

Their love dissolved my old fear.

For four decades fear had been by my side.

It was high time it let go of me.

And now I'm casting off.

I'm entrusting myself to the flow of life.

I am no longer the lame one.

The scrawny one.

The whiner.

I'm a new Aden, with a broad smile.

Standing straight in his seven-league boots.

One leg less anchored to the ground than the other, but so what?

No one notices this detail when I succeed in shoving it into the background.

I dance as I walk.

I walk as I dance.

And so I dance.

So I dance.

We dance, we dance.

When we came home at dawn, we took incredible precautions so as not to shorten your sleep. In the bathroom, for the last time, I summoned my old friends, the friends who had cradled me in their arms all my childhood. I mean fever, pain, anger, sadness and all the other states I threw myself into like a diver looking for wrecks. I cradled them in my strong arms. I cradled them one last time, gently. I said to them, firmly: 'There, your rounds are over. Forget me. And now, get out!' At that moment, I acted like Dorothy, the little heroine of *The Wizard of Oz*. Do you remember the story of Dorothy's little group who set out on a yellow brick road to reach the Emerald City? And once they got through the door, there is this terrifying monster inside, but in reality, it's just a guy hidden behind a curtain. For me, too, going on forty, the truth burst into broad daylight and

I realized that my anxiety, my anger and bitterness had no more substance than the sad sack behind his curtain who terrorized Dorothy and her friends.

After my long night of shouts, jumps, twists, coupés-décalés and pogos in the midst of the boisterous crowd in the concert hall, I felt fresh as a daisy. And very early the next day—a Sunday—I put on my athletic shoes. I ran through the neighbourhood at a speed that was neither too slow nor too fast. The only people I encountered were wearing the badges of Paris garbage collectors. Perched on small, bright green trucks, they were sweeping detritus off the sidewalk with big bursts from their water hoses. Béa, I felt truly grateful for those men who are up at dawn to provide comfort and hygiene for us.

I caught my breath at the corner of Boulevard Magenta. I was taking a deep breath of fresh air when suddenly the smell of bread and roasted almonds tickled my nostrils and then my neurons. The bakery on Rue Saint-Laurent had just opened its doors to greet its first customer. I was the next one. With croissants and baguettes under my arm, I retraced my steps. At a trot, this time. When I returned, you were asleep. And when I came out of the bathroom, shaved, dressed and perfumed, you were still asleep. I had put the croissants and the bread on the kitchen table. Very quietly... David and Abigail had gone *diretto* to the airport. I read the farewell note they left. I sat down with a tall glass of water in my hand, trying to get my bearings. My mind was in a whirl. My back was aching. Images came back and played in a loop in my head. Capering about and hips swaying in the company of Stromae, legs glued firmly to the floor or up in the air. Stromae's tunes were drilling into my noggin.

I had breakfast in silence, careful not to make noise with the dishes. Your sleep and Margherita's sleep were precious to me, Béa, even if your mother sometimes seems to doubt it. She claims I often make more noise than an elephant in a china shop.

Then I took the Metro, the Bastille line. No, let me reassure you, Béa, I did not go back to dance. The concert hall must have been closed by that time and the members of Stromae's band were snoring somewhere in a VIP hotel. I walked toward my Thai massage salon. The masseuses ran their agile fingers over my back, my chest, my legs and even over the bones of my skull. They remind me of Grandma Cochise whenever they smile at me. I miss my grandmother's laugh. It was a cascade of cool water that made you happy and at the same time quenched your thirst. I always wanted to prolong my time alone together with your great-grandmother and take advantage of her stories and wise maxims. Once in the semi-darkness of the salon, I couldn't repress that thought. The masseuses make me think of my ancestor. They have totally mastered the art of waking up the blood that has fallen asleep and turn heavy as mercury. When I walked out of the salon, I felt happy. Happy and at peace. An inner peace that I was able to feel outside of me. If I have recalled my past, if I've been through the alleys of my childhood one last time, it was to share with you my past years and their load of questions and anxieties. I hope you are now at peace, like me. When I grow old in my turn, I hope you'll share your childish fears with me. I would like to have the face of an old, serene, wise man.

I would like to present the forehead, devastated by wrinkles, of my grandmother,

the lean body of my father,

the crumpled face of my short-legged Mama

that holds the sensuality transmitted by the cobblestones of old cities,

slippery from being polished by the hurried steps of pilgrims,

agile steps,

living steps,

dancing steps, Béa, of course.

Acknowledgements

My affectionate thanks to the women who pampered me during the days, dark or luminous, of my childhood.

And my heartfelt thanks to all the banisters of stairs in buildings, in the Metro and elsewhere.

Not to forget the escalators.

And the elevators.

Support *Why Do You Dance When You Walk?*

We hope you enjoyed reading this book. It was brought to you by Cassava Republic Press, an award-winning independent publisher based in Abuja and London. If you think more people should read this book, here's how you can support:

1. **Recommend it.** Don't keep the enjoyment of this book to yourself; tell everyone you know. Spread the word to your friends and family.

2. **Review, review review.** Your opinion is powerful and a positive review from you can generate new sales. Spare a minute to leave a short review on Amazon, GoodReads, Wordery, our website and other book buying sites.

3. **Join the conversation.** Hearing somebody you trust talk about a book with passion and excitement is one of the most powerful ways to get people to engage with it. If you like this book, talk about it, Facebook it, Tweet it, Blog it, Instagram it. Take pictures of the book and quote or highlight from your favourite passage. You could even add a link so others know where to purchase the book from.

4. **Buy the book as gifts for others.** Buying a gift is a regular activity for most of us – birthdays, anniversaries, holidays, special days or just a nice present for a loved one for no reason... If you love this book and you think it might resonate with others, then please buy extra copies!

5. **Get your local bookshop or library to stock it.** Sometimes bookshops and libraries only order books that

they have heard about. If you loved this book, why not ask your librarian or bookshop to order it in. If enough people request a title, the bookshop or library will take note and will order a few copies for their shelves.

6. **Recommend a book to your book club.** Persuade your book club to read this book and discuss what you enjoy about the book in the company of others. This is a wonderful way to share what you like and help to boost the sales and popularity of this book. You can also join our online book club on Facebook at Afri-Lit Club to discuss books by other African writers.

7. **Attend a book reading.** There are lots of opportunities to hear writers talk about their work. Support them by attending their book events. Get your friends, colleagues and families to a reading and show an author your support.

Thank you!

Stay up to date with the latest books, special offers and exclusive content with our monthly newsletter.

Sign up on our website:
www.cassavarepublic.biz

Twitter/Tiktok: @cassavarepublic
Instagram: @cassavarepublicpress
Facebook: facebook.com/CassavaRepublic
Hashtag: #WhyDoYouDanceWhenYouWalk #ReadCassava

PRODUCTION CREDITS

Transforming a manuscript into the book you are now reading is a team effort. Cassava Republic Press would like to thank everyone who helped in the production of *Why Do You Dance When You Walk?:*

Publishing Director: Bibi Bakare-Yusuf

Editorial
Copy-editor: Layla Mohamed
Proofreader: Boluwatito Sanusi

Design & Production
Cover Design: Jamie Keenan
Layout: Deepak Sharma

Marketing & Publicity
Marketing and Contents Officer: Rhoda Nuhu

Sales and Admin
Sales Team: Kofo Okunola & The Ingram Sales Team
Accounts & Admin: Adeyinka Adewole